BATTLE LINE

by

LOUIS ORGAL

This book is a work of fiction. Names, characters, places and incidents are either the product of the author's imagination or are used fictitiously. Any resemblance to actual events or locales or persons, living or dead, is entirely coincidental.

ISBN: 978-0-9874946-2-7

BATTLE LINE

A continuation of the book "The Line". John and Gwen had made a comfortable life for themselves in the city of Sevilla on the planet Arieta. But it did not last long. They were discovered, pursued, and had to resort to summoning the Waps for rescue. Back through space at The Line they settled down again, but it was not to last. The Erch, the foes of the Waps, attacked human space. John was asked by his friends, the Waps, to go back to space as a liaison with the humans, as their warships tried to prevent the Erch take over human space. The Erch had got as far as Arieta, on which they had landed, but several space battles later the combined Human-Waps fleet had prevented the Erch penetrating further. Then John landed on Arieta, and inspired the population to resist. After many months of fighting in Sevilla under John's leadership the war went into reverse and the humans began pushing the Erch back. Now a hero, John was asked to go to Earth to recommence his role as adviser to the Waps in their negotiations with the humans, and was reunited, to his surprise, with Gwen and the kids. But Rick had not forgotten them!

INTRODUCTION

In the previous book, “The Line”, John and Gwen have been left on the top of a mountain on a distant inhabited planet by the Waps, with a pile of gold and some food and clothing, in return for helping them with negotiations at The Line. The Line is planet that has the sole value that it is the meeting place between humans and the Waps, a wasp like creature with a strange literal psychology, one characteristic being that they do not like being cheated in the slightest bit, and demand the death of any trader who did cheat them, even inadvertently.

The actual Line was drawn across a continent on this planet from the north to the south. It was death to cross it. The trade across the Line was extremely valuable, and the currency of exchange was bars of gold. John had taken the job of trader, risking his life, in return for making a lot of money in a short time. But his trading did not start off well. He took a girl, Gwen, who was pursued by criminals, under his wing. This made John a target, and so his firm would try to kill him as soon as they could replace him. They would do this by substituting inferior trade goods in the trade with the Waps.

However inadvertently John became friendly with his Waps trader opposite number, whom he called Fred. He accidently found that the Waps were very interested in buying milk, and he accumulated a credit with the Waps secretly selling them litre cartons of milk. When his firm eventually tried to kill him by substituting an inferior case of tea, the Waps killed John's manager instead of John. John and Gwen were then forced to step over the Line into Waps territory.

After a hectic dash back over the line next day to buy food and more milk, John was drawn into negotiations between the humans and the Waps. These negotiations started with demands that John and Gwen be returned to the human side of the line. But events caused the negotiations to evolve into resolving the main differences between the Waps and the humans. With John's help in the negotiations, describing the psychology of the humans to the Waps, and using his increasing knowledge of the Waps psychology, John and Gwen accumulated a considerable credit in gold bars with the Waps. This eventually paid for a flight in a Waps space ship through a secret wormhole in space to a human habited planet, where they were landed secretly at night on top of a mountain some ten kilometers from a town in the valley below, together with the rest of the credit, a pile of gold bars.

The story continues. Can John and Gwen move unobtrusively into this new society and hide? Would they have to run for it and summon a Waps rescue on the communication device left with them? Would the Waps leave them alone to make a new life together, or will they summon them back to help resolve further difficulties between the Waps and the humans?

CHAPTER ONE

On top of the mountain, John looked down on the twinkling lights of the town below, and noticed that dawn was breaking.

"Gwen," he said, "we will hide these ten bars of gold under the forest litter, tidy up where we buried the rest of the gold so it is hidden, grab all the food we can carry, all that cash Fred left us with, hide the rest of the food and clothing, and head down the mountain."

"Yes, John," she replied, "but you will have to stop sounding like the Waps."

John laughed. "I've got into a bad habit."

An hour later, and after a quick meal, John looked around and said, "Well, it does not look so obvious we have been here, lets go."

"What are we going to do, darling?" said Gwen. John noticed Gwen was looking at him in a new way, and coloring slightly pink. John thought, "Well if this is love, bring it on!"

"My plans overall is to buy an air vehicle as soon as we can. Not move into a hotel. But first of all we have to scout the town out. We know absolutely nothing of where we are. Who are the inhabitants? What they look like? Even if they take our money. Will they be suspicious? We will have to act like tourists and try to be inconspicuous. Try to gain as much information as we can without drawing attention to ourselves."

"Oh, dear!" said Gwen.

"Don't worry. We shall be careful, and do what I say," replied John.

"I will," said Gwen, cuddling up to him, and tweaking his nose, "But you are sounding like the Waps again."

"I'll try not to," John replied smiling, giving Gwen a cuddle.

The trip down hill was relatively easy, as long as they remained careful. The slope was lightly wooded, and eventually leveled out after about two hours struggle through the brush. They came to a fence, the other side of which were open fields.

"It looks electrified," said John, "just to keep the wild animals out. Don't worry, I know how to get through." He picked up two large sticks with small branches sticking out of them, and gingerly touched one wire. He felt nothing. He then carefully pushed the wires aside, and held them apart by positioning the sticks so that they held the wires.

"Now throw the food through," he said to Gwen, "and then carefully step through yourself without touching the wires."

They both managed to get through. John, being a bit larger was assisted by Gwen. "Thanks. Now we can take the branches out and we can continue our journey." He threw them back over the fence.

For the rest of the walk, they strolled downhill through fields and climbed over gates until they reached a rough road which led to the town, which they reached at what John felt was midday.

On the way John said, "We will leave the food just behind a hedge here. We will walk into town just looking like tourists. This small bag can carry our money, and I shall carry some too in my pockets. We shall just stroll along looking at the people and listening to their language. That won't cost us anything."

"You are beginning to think like the Waps," Gwen said smiling. John grinned.

"After we have got as much information as we can, we must then try to spend a bit of money. If they won't accept it, we will have to try to get it changed. Otherwise we will have to return to our food packages to eat while we think of what to do next."

They soon entered the town, walking by single story houses on their own plot of land. There was a mixture of air cars and land vehicles in the driveways. "Pretty standard and a relatively high standard of living. We should be able to buy an air car if our luck holds out," John thought.

They reached what appeared to be the main drag, and passed a motel, and John looked at its name. "We will claim to be booked there – Motel Estella," he said. Then he noticed that the signs were in Spanish. "Damn," he said, "but at least that reduces the chances they have heard of us."

They walked up and down the footpath along the main street. The buildings were vaguely Spanish style, with roofs over the footpath. The people had a lightly tanned skin, and clearly spoke Spanish. The signs were in Spanish. Otherwise their clothing was the same as what John and Gwen wore. "Remember we are touristas," said John to Gwen, "Lets try to buy a local newspaper at this store."

"Buenos tardes," John said to the shop girls, picking up a paper, "Com est ci? How much is this?" He handed her a five credit note. She looked at it and shook her head, and called her manager.

"Si?" he asked.

John decided to speak in Standard. "We are touristas. We have run out of your money. We need to buy a paper."

"Non, senor. You must go to ze bank," he replied and pointed.

"Muchos gracias, Senor. Buenos dias," John replied.

"Dias," replied the man.

"So much for my rotten Spanish," said John to Gwen after the left. "Lets try the bank."

The entered the bank and saw a sign "Cambio" over one counter.

"Buenos dias, nos touristas," said John, "Nous diseree exchange," and he produced a few hundred credits. The girl looked at him, and went to get a manager.

"How may I help you senor?" the manager asked.

"Oh, thank you! We wish to change some money," John said and produced a wad of hundred credit notes.

The manger immediately saw that it was a large sum and said, "We do not get many tourists down her, though it is a lovely area."

"Yes, we are visiting a friend who is up in the mountains. But to do that we need to buy an air car. But very foolishly we left all our other money behind, and the air taxi which flew us here has left."

"I am sad to hear that. You will have to pay quite a large commission, as we do not do much of this type of exchange. Please may I have your passport?"

"Passport?"

"Si. That is the requirement."

"Oh no! Did we pack our passports, darling?" said John looking at Gwen.

"Oh, darling, I left them in the hotel safe. I did not think that we would need them. And I left the money behind! Oh what are we going to do? We won't be able to eat!" and she looked at the manager imploringly, her blue eyes wide open, her hands clasped.

The manager looked at the pile of credits, and asked, "How much will you need to change?" he asked.

"Several hundred credits at least," John replied, "and I need to buy an air car."

"I'll see what I can do to help," said the manager, "but it won't be a good rate of exchange."

"Yes, that will be fine!" said John. "We will be very grateful." "Yes, we will!" enthused Gwen.

"Meet me afterwards. The bank closes in about an hour," the manager said.

It was a long hour. They hung about, and drank some water at a public fountain. Eventually they saw staff leaving the bank, and the manager appeared. The approached him and he had a big smile.

"Senor, I can help you with a few hundred Pesetas," he announced, "come over to this coffee shop."

They sat down at the table. "How many Pasetas," Jon asked. "Five hundred," the manager replied.

"And how much," asked John.

"Five hundred Credits."

"That's fine," said John, "you have been very helpful," and he counted off five hundred Credits from a roll.

"Another thing. Do you know if anyone can sell us an air car for Credits?" John asked.

"Well, Senor. I have a brother-in-law who does have a car for sale. Maybe he can be willing to sell for Credits."

"Great. Can we go there now? We really need to get moving. This friend is my uncle, and he has told us he is sick. I need to see him to settle some family arrangements."

"Senor. I will call him." And he got out his mobile phone, walked away and began talking animatedly in Spanish.

He turned back. "Si, senor. He still has the car, and can see you."

John paid for the coffee with a hundred Paseta note. He wanted to test the quality of the note and look at the type of change.

The brother-in-law was sallow and un-shaven, and looked a bit shifty. "All the better," thought John. He was located at farm a short way out of town.

The car looked old, but in reasonably good condition.

"We need to test the car. He will drive it while I am next to him, and then I will drive it while he is next to me. He needs to demonstrate if the GPS works. I don't want to get lost!!" John said.

This was done, and the man demonstrated the GPS in Spanish.

"How much?" asked John.

The manager said, "Six thousand credits."

"It sounds rather a lot, but he must not ask me for any papers. I left them behind also."

There was a further incomprehensible chat, and then the man shrugged, and gestured for the money. John counted out to him sixty hundred Credit notes.

John said, "Hop in Gwen, we have got to get going." He shook hands with the manager and his rather greasy brother-in-law, pulled the car up and headed back to town.

"Are we going to stay at that hotel," asked Gwen.

"Nope, back on top of the mountain. It is much safer."

CHAPTER TWO

The night on the mountain was not too bad. There were strange sounds in the night, some quite near. Gwen snuggled close up to him, but John felt that this was just an excuse. The car smelled of tobacco, but otherwise seemed in good working order.

John tested the GPS, and found out that they were on a planet called Arieta. They were located on the bottom left hand corner of a southern continent. The largest city of the continent, Sevilla, was not the planetary capital. Which was located on another continent in the northern hemisphere. The journey to this continental capital, which was what John decided it was, was at least two days journey by air car away. "The Waps have landed us at the most distant location they could find. They went down over the ocean. Low over the mountains. Then near this isolated town. Not bad," he mused.

"But we will have to change the gold if we are to survive," he continued to explain to Gwen. "We will load the ten bars in the car, and look for some method to change it. The five hundred Pasetas should get us to this city. Find a suitable place to stay. A bit of a spruce up. Then see how we can change gold bars."

Next day they packed the gold into the car, onto the floor in its center, then all the food and gear, and set off to the town to refuel. After that was completed, John taking great care not to go near the center of town, they picked up the food they had hidden behind the hedge, and they headed for the city.

John had worked out how to use the GPS, and he had some experience flying air cars back on his home planet. They took longer than two days because of rest stops and meals.

John and Gwen had their first difference of opinion when John insisted that they did not stay at motels. "Our money won't stretch that far," John insisted. "Also they will have a registration process. As we need to pay in cash, that will cause an automatic alert and also they will ask for a deposit. They will also take note of our car registration number. I will see if we can stay at a camp-site with a shower. But the moment they become sticky we are off."

The first town they stopped in did not have a camp-site. After a meal, they landed at a quiet place near a river, and after a bit of a wash, spent the night in the car. The next night they found a camp-site with a shower, and the camp site owner did not ask too many questions.

"Shower all you want," said John, "but it will have to be separate showers!".

The city of Sevilla was medium sized, and John followed the traffic signaling system in, and parked at a parking station. Once inside, John turned off the engine and began to take stock.

"Gwen, we have to count what we have, and then decide what we have to do," John said staring out of the windscreen.

"You've got me, dearest," replied Gwen.

"Aside from you, and you are my biggest asset," he cuddled her and pecked her on the cheek. "Now we have between thirty and forty thousand credits left, about one hundred Pesetas, one hundred kilos of gold in the car, and over two thousand buried, and some food and clothing."

He continued to think. "Our most immediate need is more Pesetas, or we will be spending more nights in the car."

"Groan," said Gwen.

"But I feel this is one of those planets which require ID for booking into a hotel. I don't know how we are going to fix that. But let's go for a walk. I'll keep a lookout and something will turn up."

They left the car, carefully locked it, and left the parking station. The street led to a major avenue, and they walked along it to what they felt was the city center. They arrived at a major square, surrounded by large impressive public buildings, banks and expensive hotels. In the center of the square was an impressive statue with fountains, and cafes. They crossed the road onto the square and John noticed a kiosk with the sign saying "Cambio, Walchen, Exchange."

"We must be in the tourist center," he said and approached the kiosk.

"Can you exchange some money for me?" John asked.

"Si, senor, how much do you wish to change?" said the man in the kiosk.

"One thousand Credits," he said, producing the notes.

"Could I have your passport please?" the man said.

"Oh damn," John said, "I have left it at the hotel."

"I am desoléé," the man said, "those are the regulations."

John turned holding the money, looking disappointed, and walked a few steps away. He heard a voice, "You have a problem, senor?"

"Yes, replied John, "I need to change money in a hurry and I have not got my passport."

"Maybe I can help you," said the man.

"Can you change money without needing a passport?" John asked.

"Maybe I can, Senor. How much do you want?"

"Well, actually we need to change five thousand Credits. Can you do that?"

The man looked to the left and right quickly. "Si, I can, but I need to get the money. Come here and wait at this café. I will be back." He led them to a café and sat them down at a small metal table and said, "I will be back soon."

The ordered coffee and waited. "We might be in luck," said John to Gwen.

Soon the man was back. "I can offer six thousand, two hundred and fifty Pasetas. Not the best exchange rate…"

"I'll take it," said John.

He exchanged the five thousand Credits for the six thousand two hundred and fifty Pasetas, making a show of counting the notes.

"Can you change another five thousand Credits for me?" John asked.

The man drew in his breath. "Si, Senor," he said.

"But maybe there is also something else you can help me with," said John.

"Si, senor, what is that?" the man asked.

"My wife and I have just had a problem hiring a car. Apparently they need driving licenses. Unfortunately we forgot to pack our driving licenses. Perhaps you can find driving licenses for us?"

"Well, senor…..maybe I could," the man said.

"I will pay well….in Credits," John said, "but I need them as soon as possible. In the next hour or so."

"I'll see what I can do," the man said, getting up.

"Make sure the photographs resemble us. You will see that my wife is blonde," John said.

"I can see that the signorina is most beautiful, and is indeed blonde. I shall return here in about two hours. I suggest that you eat here. The food is excellent. I recommend the tapas to start the meal."

He stood up, bowed and left.

"It looks as if we are going to be even more lucky," said John.

Gwen smiled and clutched his hand, "Luck. It has nothing to do with it. You manage to turn everything to your advantage. We have a saying on our home planet. If you fall down a sewer you come up covered with gold dust!"

"Well, I have one piece of luck. I am married to the most beautiful girl in the galaxy."

Gwen beamed.

They ordered lunch, and as the man said it was excellent. As they were finishing with a brandy and coffee when the man reappeared.

"I have your money, signor and signorina, and the cards," he said.

"Lets start with the money. Six thousand two hundred and fifty Pasetas you say," as John dealt out five thousand Credits,

"Now lets have a look at the Driving Licenses. I won't ask if these are genuine licenses, but they must as we say pass muster. They must work if they are used with any machines."

"Si, si, senor. They are perfect!"

"Good. How much are they?"

"A thousand Credits each, senor. They cost so much as it was done with great speed."

"They must work, at least for the next week," John said.

"Senor, you will have no trouble with them, at least for your stay on Arieta!"

"Good. Here is the money. And muchos gracias senor."

The man stood up, smiled, and left.

"Will we need him again?" asked Gwen.

"Only if we stay in this city," John replied. He looked up in the sky. "It is getting late. We cannot do anything else much today. We need to find some accommodation with secure parking."

On the square there was a large screen that could be interrogated for hotels and their prices. "We will pick a medium price hotel with its own car parking," he said, "and hopefully one which will not question our use of the driving licenses."

He found a suitable hotel on the screen, and booked a room. A map gave its location.

They went back to the parking station, collected the car and drove to the hotel. It was an older hotel that had obviously fallen on more difficult times, and was trying to keep up appearances.

The booking clerk looked at the driving licenses and looked puzzled. John put a hundred credit note on the desk. He winked at the booking clerk. "We borrowed those licenses so we don't need to use our own names. We also wish to pay in cash.

In advance." And he spread hundred Paseta notes on the desk.

"Oh, of course, senor," he said. "I will need to keep the licenses, and will return them when you leave. How long will you stay?"

"Two nights. I will need your best room."

"Si, senor. Two nights. Our wedding suite. I hope you will be happy there."

"And my car?"

"Our peon can drive it down for you."

"No need. I need to know where it is kept to get things out of it. I will drive it down myself."

"Si, senor, I shall direct you."

That night, after they both had luxuriant shower, John asked, "Shall we eat?"

"No I am too tired, and I am not hungry. Bed for me," replied Gwen.

They slept soundly until morning.

CHAPTER THREE

Next morning at breakfast, John addressed Gwen while spreading some marmalade on his buttered toast, "I hope our luck holds out. We seemed to be making good progress."

Gwen smiled at him. "You always do," she said.

"Thanks, darling. But lets review our present situation and what we need to do now. We are sleeping in a comfortable hotel. We have some temporary ID, but I don't think it will last a week, before the owners report their ID is missing."

"Why not?"

"Because the license cards could have been stolen, in which case the owners will rapidly apply for a new one, or more likely the licenses have been borrowed from look-a-likes for a price for maybe a week. In either case we will not have permanent ID."

"Next," he continued, "we have plenty of the local currency. Enough for now. And a lot of gold locked in our car." He stuck the piece of toast in his mouth. "But there are two, really three things we need to do as a matter of urgency. First, decide on permanent name for each of us, and somehow get ID for it. Second sell some of the gold. And with it get a bank account. And with that get a credit card. The list gets longer and longer."

"But there is one thing we can do, or you can do, and I am leaving the most important task to you," he smiled and looked at Gwen, who looked shocked. "You have to decide what names we want."

"Why me?"

"Because you have to live with it, be happy with those names, and you are very good at deciding that sort of thing." He smiled. "We have to change our first names and our surnames. If we are going to be husband and wife, in this society we need to have the same surname. And as they will be looking for someone with our first names, we need to change that too."

"Oh," she said.

"Think about it. There is no great hurry."

John continued chewing, while Gwen raised her coffee cup and looked at him over it.

"Now how are we going to sell the gold?" he asked.

"Could we use that gentleman again?" Gwen asked.

"I thought of that, but I think it would be beyond his capacity, and I doubt if he is completely honest. What we need is a regular seller of gold. I suspect that is difficult enough on this planet. And we would need a legitimate ID and cover for our possession of gold. We seem to be again stuck. If only we could get some advice. Some competent person who would know what to do and do it for us.

And maybe get us a legitimate ID through him as well."

"Maybe you need a lawyer!" Gwen said gaily.

"Gwen, you are a genius!" exclaimed John.

"What! I wasn't serious."

"Yes you were. That idea is brilliant. We will get the top lawyer in the city, who will charge us a bomb, but sell the gold for us, and also open a bank account that will provide us a credit card. That should provide us with sufficient ID. I am sure he can fix for us any further ID's which are necessary," John replied.

"You're kidding!"

"Nope. That is the way to go."

"But I now need our new names. What surname do you want? Sorry to press you."

"Oh dear! Let me think." Gwen mumbled to herself. "Brown. What do you think of Brown?"

"Lovely. Now you have got to change your first name, and nothing beginning with G. And what name do you want for me, not beginning with J."

She thought. "I have always liked Emmaline. What do you think of that?"

"Lovely! I shall call you Emma. And mine?"

Hmmm. "Peter?"

"Great. We are now Senor Peter Brown and Senora Emmaline Brown. Remember that. Write it down before you forget."

John approached the manager of the hotel. “Senor, I need your advice.” He produced a hundred Peseta note. “The lady and I are strangers in this city, but we have decided that we need a good lawyer. You know how it is. Certain personal difficulties. We wish to employ the best and most reputable lawyer in town. I know it is expensive but our needs are great. Which is the most prestigious law farm in town, and who is the top lawyer there?”

“There are many good law firms..” the manager began, but John waved his hundred Paseta note and produced another one. The manager licked his lips and continued, “The most prestigious is José de Silva and Co, and their senior partner is, let’s see, and he referred to a screen in his desk, Senor Raymond Henrique.”

“Could you be kind enough to contact him and make an appointment for us, please?”

“In whose name, Senor?”

“Senor Peter Brown, but this is confidential, you understand,” handing him the notes.

“Si, Senor.”

The appointment was at 11 in the morning.

John said, “We need to tidy up, grab a couple of gold bars from the car, and take a cab. It’s a pity we can’t take more, but ten kilos each is the maximum we can carry. I shall ask reception if they can supply us with a couple of carry bags.”

They arrived at the office building in the center of the city in plenty of time, and went up to the sixth floor. “Senor and Senora Brown to see Mr

Raymond Henrique." She gave them an odd look, but they were ushered in a few minutes later.

Senor Henrique also gave them an odd look. He was a thick set man, wearing an expensive suit, and well cut white hair. Before he could say anything John put the two gold bars on his desk and set, "I suggest that you use the electric lock to lock the door. And when your receptionist rings in a few minutes to say Senor Smith needs to see you, tell her you are busy."

"I assume you have many more of these gold bars," the lawyer said.

"Yes, many more."

He touched a button on the desk and there was a click in the door, and when his secretary rang a few minutes later he told her he would deal with the matter later.

"So, how can I help you?" he asked.

"We want you to sell these two gold bars, and many others we provide you later. We want you to open a bank account for us and pay this money into it, and we want you to obtain from the Bank a debit card for each of us. That will do for the moment. You can of course deduct whatever commission you deem necessary."

"I see. And what are your names, Senor?"

"My name is Peter Brown and my wife is Emmaline Brown. I have written the names here along with your instructions."

"You say you have other gold bars?" the lawyer said.

"A lot more, but as you may realize, the reason for coming to you is to have the transaction completely confidential."

"I see, I shall see what I can do."

"When do you think you can sell them?"

"I shall let you know in a couple of days."

"Good. I am staying at the Excelsior Hotel. But I shall contact you in a couple of days. I just need a receipt for the two gold bars."

"Senor, I do not know if they are gold. I will give you a receipt for two bars with these numbers on."

"Fine. Now if you satisfy us we will have a lot more work for you to do for us."

"I shall endeavor to provide a good service." The lawyer wrote out the receipt, and then rose and showed them out past the staring secretary and receptionist.

"Well, so far so good," said John, as they left the building, "lets go to this café and have more of this excellent coffee."

"Do you think he will sell the gold," asked Gwen.

"Yes, but I don't know how long it will take. But the time is not very important. We can stay at the hotel for another three nights, then back to the car for us if necessary."

Gwen did not say anything. She smiled and placed her hand on his.

"So let's think," said John, "we have the gold pretty well squared away, I think. That will give us heaps of money. And we will have a bank account. So what is the next priority."

He sat there musing, staring out at the square, the same large square that that had met the man yesterday.

"This looks a nice place," said John, looking at the fountains, people and restaurants. "If we get a pile of money, how about staying here?"

"Here?' replied Gwen, "Well, OK, I have no objections."

"Well it is a good location to hide in. An isolated planet, an isolated continent, and the city looks a comfortable place to stay."

"Suits me!" said Gwen, smiling and placing both her hands on his.

"Right, Sevilla will be our home!" said John.

Just at that point, Gwen said, "Look, there is that man again!"

John looked and saw him walking around the square obviously trying to pick up more tourists. A thought struck him. Maybe this man will be of further use to them. What they needed was permanent ID. Maybe the man would help them get it.

"Come on, Gwen, we need to talk further with this man," John said, suddenly getting up. Gwen got up without a word, John paid the bill, and they hurried across the road onto the square and hurried after the man.

"Buenos sera! How are you today?" John said smiling.

The man gave a start, and then said, "May I be of more service to you?"

"Yes, you may. Perhaps you can have a lunch with us. You will get a free lunch and after you have discussed with us what we want, you will have no obligation if you refuse. Non obligado."

"Oh. You were happy with my services yesterday?"

"Si. No problema. We just want more. Which is a good restaurant for lunch."

"Well, senor, here Alfredos is really good. The tapas are excellent." He was already looking hungry.

They sat down and ordered. Soon an excellent meal and even better wine arrived. After a bit of chit-chat John asked his name. "Alfredo, like this restaurant," the man replied.

"Well," said John, "my name is Peter and my wife's name is Emma."

"Peterr and Emma, that is good," Alfredo replied.

"Well, Alfredo, we like this city, and we have decided to stay," John said.

"Here in Sevilla, bueno!" Alfredo replied.

"However we have a problem. To stay we need permanent identities. Much better than those driving licenses."

"But senor, wealthy people like you will have no difficulties. Just apply, show your passports, and you will have no problem!" said Alfredo surprised.

"But we want local identification papers, genuine ones, without approaching the authorities," John replied.

Alfredo began to look afraid. "You are in trouble?"

"We won't go into that. We have not broken the law. But we have travelled far because powerful people want to harm us." John clutched Gwen's hand.

Alfredo's eyes shifted to Gwen.

"You wish to remain hidden?"

"Si. We wish to remain together in Sevilla. We will not break any laws. We will live quietly here. But maybe you can be of service to us?"

"I see…You will need an identification card. Everyone has to have one. We must produce it if the police ask. It has a photograph and the DNA numbers on it. It is impossible to forge."

"Yes. But how do you get one? A legitimate one?"

"You must apply, senor."

"In person?"

"Non, senor, that is not necessary. We sometimes use compradores, agents, for these sort of things, especially if you are rich."

"We are rich." John smiled. "What must you have to apply?"

"Senor, the form completed, of course, several photographs signed by a notary, saying that the photograph is correct, a blood sample for the DNA, and your birth certificate."

"Can an older person apply for this ID?"

"Si, if you move residences you must apply for a new identity card."

"Hmmm, so the way I see it is, aside from your services, we just need birth certificates."

"Well….si senor….but you have no Arietan birth certificates."

"That is an additional service you can provide. You must obtain for us birth certificates for persons our age," John said, " and they must not have been used before."

"How am I going to do that?"

"Alfredo, you must find a male and female of our age whose births were registered, and died in childhood. We will be happy with any name you can find. You obtain copies of their birth certificates. Then you apply for the cards in the normal manner. I'll leave it to you to arrange the notaries." John smiled.

Alfredo considered. "It will cost a lot of money."

"I know. I will pay you two thousand Credits in advance. More when the job is completed. One other thing. You can provide us with an immediate necessary service. We need two mobile phones. How much do you think they will cost do you think?"

"How good mobile phones?"

"Good ones. You decide."

"Five hundred credits each," Alfredo said.

"Here you are, one thousand credits. You will get the other two thousand credits when you return," John said.

Alfredo finished his meal and left, while Gwen and John sat there enjoying their pastis.

Soon Alfred returned with two boxes. The contained two satellite phones. John said "I'll just check if the work." He rang Gwen. "Hello." "I love you," John said. Gwen looked into his eyes and blushed.

"Well, Alfredo, here is two thousand Credits. I am paying you also for your loyalty. If you do good work for me, you will be well paid. You will be, what is the word, my comprador."

"Si, senor," replied Alfredo, "I will be happy to be your comprador."

CHAPTER FOUR

John and Gwen settled into life in the city of Sevilla on the planet Arieta. They received genuine identity passes with Spanish names from Alfredo, sold one hundred 10 kilo bars of gold through the lawyer, bought a large house, and as respected and wealthy citizens of their new city set up an investment bank to invest in property and businesses.

The other bars of gold they deposited in a bank, in safe custody.

They got married officially and soon had two children, Hugh and Emmaline. As Gwen said, if I can't be Emmaline, my lovely girl will be. John suspected that at the speed of Hugh's arrival, Gwen might have already been pregnant when they had arrived on the planet, though she had not mentioned it. In private they still called each other Gwen and John, and they explained to the children that this was the English version of their Spanish names.

Five years later.........

John was first aware that the authorities had found them when he received a phone call from Alfredo.

"Senor Peter, many federales have entered the city. They have been enquiring after John and Gwen. These are the names you told me to listen for."

"Many thanks, Alfredo. You have done well. Now you and your family must disappear, and be gone for many months. You have prepared for this. You have much money I have put in a special account for you for this. Go and take a holiday."

"Si, senor. I go." He rang off.

He was just about to ring Gwen when he received another phone call from the lawyer's secretary. "Senor Brown, many police have entered Senor Henrique's office. They are shouting at him about gold. You asked me to ring you if this happens."

"Thank you, Phillipé. Now remember, you know nothing. But as soon as they take him away, ring the most senior judge you know and tell them what has happened."

"Si Senor Brown".

John rang Gwen on the special tiny phone hanging around her neck. "Abracadabra!" he shouted.

"What?" said Gwen.

"Abracadabra! You know what that means. Tie the kids into the getaway car, and I will be there in ten minutes."

He grabbed signed instructions from his desk, and ran past Rose, his secretary. "Date stamp those signed instructions and distribute them. I have to go."

"Senor, when will you be back?"

"I will return, but it will be a long while!" shouted John, as he headed for the stairs to the roof and his car.

He arrived at his home on the top of a hill in ten minutes. He had bought priority traffic rights for his car.

He leapt out and ran to the special garage, and saw Gwen arguing with the nanny. He shoved the nanny back, yelled "You will be looked after!" and pushed Gwen and the children through a thick metal door and locked it behind them. "I told you to have them strapped in." He nudged her in the backside with his knee. "Hurry!"

Gwen squeaked to complain. She had become more matronly after two children, and a life of luxury had slowed her down. John just opened the car door, picked up Hugh, and began to strap him in hurriedly. Gwen quickly grabbed Emma, and strapped her in on the other side surprisingly quickly.

After they had got in themselves, John looked at the monitors on the wall of the garage. "Damn! They have arrived already, " he said, as he saw police cars draw up. "This will have to be a quick getaway."

He turned round. "Hold tight!" he yelled, gunned the engine, pressed a button, and the garage doors blew off. The air car screamed out of the garage and up into the air, scattering the cops.

John looked in the rear screen. The police were already racing for their cars. He did not waste time climbing. He screamed over roofs accelerating to maximum speed, then down nearly to the surface of a wide river and headed west. He switched on automatic pilot. "This will keep them confused," he said, as the air car started following the land contours closely on a pre-planned course, ducking behind hills.

"Will they catch up with us?" asked Gwen.

"Eventually, yes," said John, "they will track us with satellites. But we should reach the mountains first. We will get into a valley, slow down, and switch on the cloaking device. From then on they won't know if we go north or south."

John began to track his pursuers on the screen. "They will fall behind as they can't see us. But when they get satellite direction they will head straight for us."

He watched the blips and the map, and sure enough the blips slowly began to catch up. "I can't afford to switch off the automatic pilot," he thought, "I will just hope that they don't reach us before we get the mountains."

A bit over an hour later they reached the mountains, shot over a ridge, and down into a valley on the other side and slowed. "Cloaking on," said John, pressing a switch. The air car continued over another ridge and then turned south, and continued at a slower speed as the car climbed and descended. "Its pity this device does not work faster than 100k," John thought. He checked the screen. The pips jumped into the next valley, went on for a while, then moved around in a confused manner.

"Well, that's dropped you," he said.

"Are we safe now," asked Gwen.

The kids chimed in, "Are we there yet?"

"Yes we are safe, but we are not there yet. Kids, next to your seats are sweeties, drinks, and games. We have a long way to go. We can have brief stops along the way, as long as you don't go far from the car. "

"Where are we going, Dad?" asked Hugh.

"Somewhere safe," John replied.

"Were they bad men after us?" asked Hugh.

"Yes, very bad men," replied John.

"I don't like bad men," announced Emma.

The air car continued south along a mountain chain along the west side of the continent, climbing mountains and ducking down into valleys. Counting a few rest stops, they arrived at the mountain destination, the planned space-ship pickup point, early next morning. The car arrived at the rear of the mountain and stopped above some trees. "I'll take control now," said John. He carefully guided it at ground level to the familiar clearing at the top of the mountain.

"Nobody get out. We are not staying," he said, got out and grabbed grav pack from the luggage compartment.

He strapped it on, said "Here goes," and gently floated up the side of a large conifer tree. The signal unit was still there. "I hope this works," he said to himself and pulled the red handle. There was a clunk, a hum, but nothing else happened.

He flew back down, repacked the grav pack in the car, and said to Gwen, "We have six nights to wait without being caught. We will now hide the car."

As per their careful plan, they then waited in the trees well away from the mountaintop until dark. The cloaking unit was still humming away and the green light winking.

They then proceeded silently to the locked mountain shed they had hired from the greasy farmer that they had bought a car from when they had arrived on the planet. They landed, John applied his thumb to the lock, and they moved the car inside.

"OK Gwen, we'll move everything from the car to the grav raft, strap the kids on, cover it with the camouflage covering, and we will get out of here!" John locked the door behind him. "I hope our pal does not get nosy," he thought.

"According to the map, there is a river a few K's away in the forest, and a place with a canyon and overhanging rocks. We will camp there." They both carefully floated the raft, Gwen and John wearing grav packs, until they reached this destination. "If we are careful we won't be spotted by satellites," John said.

Part way through the afternoon on the last day, they carefully loaded backpacks with food. "I don't know if we will starve, but with Hugh and Emma we won't risk it." The dumped everything else they did not need, including Gwen's designer dress. She had already donned pants and a shirt. She had been strangely quiet for the five days, just watching the kids intently.

They quietly floated the raft up the side of the mountain. They arrived just when the light was failing.

John pulled out a pair of small binoculars and observed the town below. “Damn, the town appears infested with police or troops. They must be really making an effort to catch us. Tuck under the camouflage material and lie still.”

It was all quiet. “I hope they stop searching at night,” thought John.

Round about midnight they saw a dark shadow descend from the sky.

“Now,” whispered John. They each grabbed a child, and encumbered with their backpacks ran desperately for the landing spot. A door opened, and a light appeared. There was a shout far behind them. John pushed Gwen and Emma through the door, followed by Hugh. He leapt in himself, while a red laser blast hit the roof of the port. The door closed.

A Waps was there. He gestured to two padded seats. “Sit. Strap in,” were his brief instructions. John and Gwen threw themselves on the seats, desperately holding on to Emma and Hugh. The craft began rising, even before they had attached the buckles.

A voice announced. “There will be disturbance.”

The craft dived, straightened, then turned up and accelerated. John and Gwen desperately held onto the children. Emma began to whimper.

"More disturbance." The craft jumped sideways. Emma screamed. Hugh clung tightly. Gwen went bright red.

"The craft will dock with another," said the voice. "Stay where you are until told."

Eventually there was a clanking sound and a thump, and there was another feeling of acceleration, though this time there was some measure of inertia and gravity damping. Strange noise and thumps, and then there was a jump through a wormhole.

"Stay where you are," the voice announced again. There was more acceleration and they jumped through another wormhole.

"You may detach now," said the voice. A Waps appeared and said, "I will conduct you to your accommodation." They entered a small cabin.

"I am sorry but there is no shower," said the Waps.

CHAPTER FIVE

As soon as the Waps had gone Gwen turned on John and said furiously, "Don't you risk the lives of my children ever again!"

"But Gwen! If I left you behind you know what would have happened to you. They would have shoved a needle behind your eyeball and turned your mind to mush. Then they would have said, "Oh, these poor children! We will have to put them into care.""

Gwen turned away from him and said to Emma, "Are you hungry darling?" "Who's that man," asked Hugh. "Yes," said Emma, "He looks like an insect. A big insect! " "Insect! Insect!" yelled Hugh excitedly.

John pulled out some food bars from a pack to quiet them. "If we go carefully these should last ten days." But the Waps did indeed have a spare human food supply, enough for two of them at least.

The Waps representative soon returned and said, "I see that you have children. We did not know this. We have adequate food and water. The trip will take about ten days. We will try to avoid contact with more human ships."

John refrained from asking if they had been shot at. "We are very grateful that you risked your lives to rescue us," he started.

The Waps replied, "You are valuable to us. It is likely that we would have summoned you soon."

"Why? What has happened?"

"After you left, the relationship with humans went well for three years, and then deteriorated. We do not understand why. We do not feel we were at fault. We are now again verging on armed conflict. When we land your contact Fred can explain it to you, better than I can. I am just the commander of the ship, given the task of carrying you safely back to The Line."

After they landed they were greeted by Fred. "I am glad to see you again. I see you have bred and have children. I am pleased. Come with me and I will take you to your accommodation, which I hope you will find comfortable. I will explain what has happened at your apartment."

They were whisked from the spaceport to the Waps city on the Line, and drew up beside a building. "This building was built in human style to accommodate human visitors. They found it very comfortable, and we followed their suggestions to improve their comfort."

They entered, and Gwen and John found a large modern apartment, furnished with human furniture, containing a lounge, kitchen, two bedrooms and a bathroom, with a human type toilet, shower, bath and basins. "Are you happy?" asked Fred.

"Yes, of course," answered John, "it looks very comfortable."

"If you want more, you can ask for it," said Fred.

"Now, for an explanation…." said Fred.

"I am sorry Fred," said Gwen, "I need to put the children to bed. Can you come back in say two hours?"

"Yes," said John, "these two are our first priority."

"Understood," said Fred, "I shall return in two hours."

In exactly two hours Fred returned, after Gwen had fed the children with food she had found in the refrigerator, washed them and tucked them into the two beds she found in the second bedroom.

"So, Fred, what has happened," asked John.

"After you left, things proceeded well. Trading went well, including milk purchases, and the military negotiations were friendly. We managed to get a mutual reduction in battle ships resident in the system."

"Then things began to go wrong. For the first two years the arbitration went well. What differences were minor and were rapidly settled. Then as part of your suggested agreement, the three arbitrators on each side were replaced. Among the new arbitrators, one proved troublesome. He did not provide rapid judgments. He said he was "reserving his judgments", and soon there were a large number of disputes unsettled. At the same time he began showing gross bias to the human side, especially for your firm, Albrecht and Company, which began to provide more inferior products. As you suggested we ceased to use him, and just selected the other two arbitrators. He got angry, and somehow got the other two arbitrators to temporarily cease work. He felt the work should be shared equally. Arbitration, and indeed trade, slowed to a crawl. When this happened, we followed your final instructions how to deal with this, announced that arbitration was not working, and requested that the man, you call Rick, who shot at us in the court, should be returned to the court for summary justice. The underperforming arbitrator was very angry, and started shouting that he would get the home government to deal with it. Two days later he was found dead, and the two other arbitrators returned, as you described very chastened, and we had no trouble with the arbitration system since."

"Yes, obviously Rick's father, the criminal boss, dealt with the recalcitrant arbitrator. The other firms were glad to get rid of him too. So what next?"

"We have had trouble over the pricing of the milk."

"Did they try to increase the price of the milk, or withhold supply?" asked John.

"Occasionally, but we were not concerned. As you told us, we could rapidly get a supply from alternative sources. No; what happened was a bit more complex. As you arranged, we had negotiators regularly crossing the line. For over two years we bought all the milk they could supply at the average price we arranged with you of one kilo of gold for one liter of milk. Everyone was happy."

"Then," continued Fred, "we did not need more milk than the quantity provided."

"You mean you stopped buying milk above a fixed amount. What happened to the price?"

"Nothing at first. But we then started receiving offers to supply cheaper milk, if the orders were switched to these suppliers."

"Oh, dear!"

"Naturally we switched to buying the milk at the cheaper price. Soon others started making similar offers at lower and lower prices. We were happy at first, but the humans got very angry. They said that we were "gouging" and pitting one human off against the other to get the cheapest price. They tried to stop the supply, and sell to us at only a fixed price, but always we soon received offers to supply cheaper milk. We did not know what to do."

"Yes, I can see what happened. It is what is called a "step function" I learned in economics at school. Rationally the humans should be happy to sell at the lower price, but as you know, humans are not rational."

"We are trying to offer everyone a higher price, but that does not make them happy either," Fred continued.

"Ok, what else? Tell me the worst."

"We had an agreement that most battle ships be withdrawn from the system. But after these other troubles started, an extra battleship would enter the system. "Only temporary" they said. So after a particularly long stay of one battleship, we brought one of ours in. Soon the number in the system increased back to the old level. The humans blamed us for what they called the breakdown in the agreement. We are back to where we started, except for the military negotiating building north of the city."

"Well, Fred, we have a lot to do."

"There is even worse news," said Fred, "As you know we have other ways into human space. Until our rescue of you we believed the human's were not aware of that. On the other side of the wormhole that leads to this system, they have a large fleet, which they have been adding to. We have them under observation."

"Oh, oh!" cried John.

"Is that a word of surprise," asked Fred.

"No, concern. As soon as word reaches the fleet that the Waps can get behind them, they will panic. They can do anything. Oh, shit! I should have thought of this! Maybe trying to hide on the planet Arieta was not better than starting a war!" said John, putting his hands over his eyes.

Gwen interjected, "Oh, no!"

"This matter is serious. I shall warn our battle fleet," said Fred.

"Tell them not to do anything visible to humans immediately. I shall have to think about it. I need some rest. I will think about it." John rose.

"Fred, I shall see you at the ninth hour tomorrow morning."

"Understood. You need rest, and you are under pressure," said Fred.

"You said it," said John, showing him to the door.

CHAPTER SIX

The next day at exactly the ninth hour Fred reappeared. "Were you comfortable and did you sleep well?"

"Yes, but we noticed that in the fridge there was no milk," John replied.

Fred froze, clicked his limbs, and hummed.

"Why do you need milk?" he asked.

"We feed it to our children, and we have a bit ourselves sometimes," John replied.

"I understand. That is why humans consume so much milk. I will immediately get you some. How much do you need?"

"About six liters for the near future. But I have a plan to obtain a free regular supply for ourselves."

"But first I have given some thought on your problem. I think I can solve it and the military problem at the same time," John continued.

"This is very good," said Fred, "I am always amazed that you come up with these solutions. Were you thinking about it for a long time?

"No, I just slept on it," replied john, "And the solution just popped into my head while I was in the shower."

"What do you mean slept on it?"

"When humans sleep, half the time is spent on deep restful sleep, and half the time thinking. If we do not have major problems, we just dream, which are random thoughts and stories. My mind was thinking about the problem all through the night while I was sleeping."

"This information is very interesting. We also have a sleep state, but not for long. Just to rest the mind and body, and conduct repairs. I can see this sleeping is very useful for you."

John continued. "On the question of solving your problem, I have decided that it is best to form a cartel. I remembered my economics lessons. A cartel is a small group of sellers selling at the same price and dividing the market between them. Humans like to divide the market between them, and not compete. This way the sellers get higher prices. I thought it would be best to divide the market between the four largest firms, and raise the price of milk. The higher fixed price of milk would please them very much."

"I can see that," said Fred, "but how will this advantage us."

"Firstly, humans will accept the market being divided among a cartel. There may be complaints among the minor firms, but as these arrangements are normal in human society these complaints will not be major. The members of the cartel themselves will deal with it. So your bad relations over the milk issue will die down."

"Second," continued John, "I am sure the military problems are related to the bad relations over the milk issue. You can make it a condition that for the cartel to continue the military situation reverts to the agreed levels."

"Thirdly, and this is for both our benefits, I will make it a condition that one of the firms delivers one liter extra a day for free, and that liter will be randomly selected from that daily delivery and given to us."

John turned to Gwen and asked, "Will one liter a day be enough, darling?"

"Yes," replied Gwen, "that should be enough. And while you are both talking to me, I have prepared here a list of our needs while you are talking. Starting with kids underwear. Delivery today please." She handed the list to Fred.

Fred seemed to chuckle. "I will do my best."

"I would prefer to go across and do my own shopping," said Gwen.

"No! No!" protested John, "they will grab you!"

"So I am stuck in this apartment with the kids," said Gwen.

"Look Gwen, it is too dangerous to walk around even on the Waps side. Remember what happened to the human diplomats. The kids could run away from you. Please be reasonable."

"Huh," she said.

Fred said, "I agree with John. Maybe we can arrange some exercise well away from the city."

Gwen did not look at all mollified.

Fred said, "It appears that your mate is not happy."

"That is true," replied John, "My actions have threatened the lives of her children. It will take her a while to forgive me."

"Now," continued John, "the last important issue. How much are you prepared to pay the cartel members for the milk? It will have to be a higher price."

"What do you suggest?" asked Fred.

"I suggest a half way price if you can possibly afford it. Half a kilo of gold for each liter of milk."

"We will consider that and let you know. "

"If you wish to proceed with this suggestion, perhaps you can arrange a meeting on this side of the Line tomorrow. The meeting will be with the most senior persons in each of the four largest firms. Just one each, myself and yourself. Do you have a suitable meeting place?"

"Yes, we now have a meeting place for these meetings. I will let you know if we decide to follow your suggestion, and we can arrange such a meeting."

"However," continued Fred, "when they realize you have returned, won't they realize Waps can penetrate human space?"

"They may suspect it, but if they ask me directly, I will deny it. I will say we have dwelt on a Waps world. Those who see me won't ask, as it is not in their interest to do so. And the humans will have no evidence that it was me on Arieta, so they won't press the matter."

"Human psychology is peculiar," said Fred. He turned to go.

Gwen called, "And don't forget my milk, and the shopping list."

"And can you get me a reader, please. I wish to catch up on the news," said John.

"All will be delivered," said Fred, "What is your term? Post haste!"

As soon as Fred was gone, Gwen rounded on John. "How long will we be stuck here? While you are off solving the galaxy's problems, I am stuck here in this apartment looking after the children. Indefinitely. I can't even move outside!" She began to cry.

"Oh Gwen. This is not my fault and you know it. Cheer up. I will try to get us back to Arieta as soon as I can. I will. You know that!" She continued to weep. He cuddled her. "You were not like this when we were last here on this side of the Line. You were cheerful even when I had to leave you alone in that small apartment for the day. And you were very happy at Arieta. Cheer up. Things will get better. You know that!"

"Oh, John!" she sobbed. "Do you think you can get us out within the next nine months?"

"I am sure. But why nine months? Oh oh! You are not.....?"

"Yes," Gwen sniffled, "You are going to have another little one."

"Oh, Gwen!" John swept her up and sat her on his knee. "How wonderful. You wonderful girl!" He gave her a squeeze. ""I'll do my damndist to get us out of here before then." He then continued in a more sober tone. "I shall also increase the milk supply."

Gwen calmed down, John gave her a kiss, they held hands, cuddled, and then played with the children until Fred returned about mid day.

"I have arranged a supply of milk. It will arrive soon. I have also commenced discussions with the four largest firms. They won't be able to supply their senior representative until day after tomorrow. The items on Gwen's list are currently being purchased, and I have been promised that most items will be delivered this evening."

"I had better discuss our credit balance," said John. "How much is there?"

"About eight hundred kilos, give and take your current debits and additions. After you left your credit balance was continued to be added to as the benefits from your final actions accrued. See, I am using your accounting terms! Anyway, have no fear that you are likely to run out of credit."

"Look, Fred. This apartment, while it is very comfortable for two adults, is small for two children also. They need exercise outside a building every day. How much would it cost if you built a detached house somewhere out in the desert, with what we call a garden, an open area surrounded by a wall. The children can play and exercise in this outside open area, while being supervised and protected," asked John.

"This is unusual. We do not have such separate buildings, as we do not live with our mates and offspring. We know that other species we have met do live like this." At this point John thought "This is getting interesting." Fred continued, "What sort of design would you like for this house?

John glanced at Gwen. "The people who design houses for humans are called architects. Maybe there are some on the human side of the line. Maybe you can allow Gwen to talk to a selection of these by video-phone. She could select one, and they could design a suitable house at our expense. We could price its construction. If the cost is inside our credit, a house could be built to this design somewhere out in the desert."

Fred hummed. "Is this what you really want?"

"Yes," said John, "Gwen is already going crazy being cooped up here. She would certainly like to talk to other humans on the phone. And also give the children more exercise. We will have to think of how to do that in the short term."

"Yes," said Fred, "I will see what I can do on both issues."

After Fred left, Gwen said, "Oh, John, what is this building me a house?"

"You are going to build the house. It will keep you occupied. Even if it is unfinished when we get out of here. We will also try to arrange trips out to the desert. But you must promise me one thing. You must never, never, try to cross the Line." He looked in here eyes and held her hand. "You must promise me that!"

She melted and fell into his arms. "Oh John! Yes, of course I do. I will never try to go anywhere without you! I will never leave you!"

John cuddled her and patted her bottom. "Yes, we seem to be fated to be together always, whatever happens," he said and kissed her.

Two days later, on the way to the meeting room by car, Fred explained to John that the four firms selected for the cartel were Albrecht and Company, Union Pharmaceuticals, Ling Tam and Company, and Fisk Trading. "I know Albrecht is your old employer, and they tried to kill you," Fred said, "But they are the largest firm and the one which has traded with us for the longest time."

"That doesn't make me like them," responded John. "They are ruthless and amoral from top to bottom. However I will talk to them and make them the same offer I make the others."

Fred and John entered the meeting room first. There were four human chairs facing them. Soon four humans entered the room. Four suited men of middle aged appearance. The door closed behind them. Their eyes opened with surprise when they saw John.

"I am John Griffin. Please sit down," said John, "and introduce yourselves. You may call my colleague Fred."

The representative of Albrecht and company spoke first. "So, you have returned!" His face twisted and he gave John a steely gaze.

"Indeed," replied John, smiling thinly, "please introduce yourself."

"I am John Waterstone, and I am Chief Executive Officer of Albrecht and Company."

"I am Johannes Pizzey, CEO of Union Pharmaceuticals," the next man said in a faint German accent.

"Neville Ong, CEO of Ling Tam."

"Willard Jackson, CEO of Fisk Trading."

"I won't resort to pleasantries," said John "The Waps are unhappy with the milk supply situation and the accompanying unpleasantries. They wish to offer a cartel. They wish to divide the arrangements for milk supply between your four firms only. You will each have an equal share of the milk supply. I will turn to the Waps representative for confirmation of this proposal."

"Yes, that is our proposal. We will divide the supply of milk equally between each of your four firms. It is what you call a cartel. We will refuse all offers from alternative suppliers at lower prices."

The four men looked at John and Fred with stony faces.

John continued. "We also offer a standard price for all milk supplies of one half kilo of gold per liter, depending on quality and subject to arbitration."

The men looked stunned.

"However there are a couple of conditions attached," John continued. The men shifted uncomfortably. "First, the military situation must revert to what it was agreed to be after the negotiations, before they regressed. I believe it was one ship each in orbit around this planet."

"But we have no influence on the military!" the man from Union Pharmaceuticals protested.

"I think you do," said John, looking squarely at the Albrecht representative. "You all four now have a strong incentive to jointly maintain the status quo! I am sure you will manage to do that!"

"And how do you think we will do that?" asked the man from Albrecht and Company in a sarcastic voice.

"Well," said John, "In your firm's case, if there is a transgression maybe your firm's boss, Johannes Albrecht, will be found garroted. He has lived over a hundred years, which is long enough."

The other three men smiled wolfishly at the man from Albrecht and Company, who went bright red.

John continued. "And there is a second minor requirement. I require one of you, lets see," and he remembered the firm next door to his original trading building, who seemed a pretty decent lot, "Union Pharmaceuticals. You will supply two extra liters a day of full cream milk for my personal use, free of cost, this milk being randomly selected from your milk supply. Thus your milk supply will be the total cartel supply daily plus two liters, until further notice. You may ask why should you do this. Well, just to keep me happy." John smiled at the Union Pharmaceutical representative.

"You will decide among yourselves if you agree to this proposal, which includes the immediate military reduction. You will then jointly contact the Waps representative Fred, and discuss how the milk supply arrangements can be instituted. I am sure that you have recorded all this, so I don't need to repeat."

"Any questions?"

"Are you staying at the Line for long?" asked the Union Pharmaceuticals representative.

"As long as is necessary, and to make sure other problems do not crop up."

The four men rose, three of them nodded to John, and walked through the door.

"Do you think that they will accept," asked Fred.

"Done deal. But you must keep to your side of the bargain, or the battleships will be back," said John.

"We will certainly endeavor to do so," replied Fred.

CHAPTER SEVEN

A couple of days later Fred came in to see John and Gwen. “We have arranged a large vehicle with suitable modifications to take you out in the desert for your children to exercise.”

“Hurray!” said John, “new clothes,” referring to a previous clothing delivery, “and now we can get out into the sunshine, and have a bit of a walk.” The children began yelling and running around.

“Maybe we can have a picnic!” suggested Gwen.

“What is that?” asked Fred.

“We take food with us and have lunch in the desert,” Gwen said.

“How long can the car driver take us on this trip?” asked John.

The was a humming sound and the Fred answered, “Up to six hours, with consideration for safety.”

“Can we do that today?”

“Yes,” answered Fred.

“I will prepare the food and drink,” said Gwen gaily, rushing for the kitchen.

“There is another separate issue,” said Fred.

“What’s that, Fred?” said John.

"People want to meet you," said Fred.

"What people, and why?" asked John.

"A large number of different people, for different reasons."

Hmmm. "Tell them to specify in writing why they want to meet me. Unless you want me to meet them, I see no reason why I should meet any. I will give them all my consideration."

"There is one man we do want you to meet," replied Fred.

"Who is this, and why?" asked John.

"Johannes Albrecht."

"You mean the founder and major owner of Albrecht and Company?" John asked.

"That is correct. He says that he wishes to see you out of curiosity and for personal reasons."

"Oh. Do you think I should?" asked John.

"Yes. You may not think we have personal relationships with humans, but for a long time we have had one with Mr Albrecht. He is one of the few, like you, who seems to understand us. Also he was the human who originated trading with our species. At great personal danger to himself."

"Oh. How did he do it?" asked John.

"He landed his ship on one of our planets. Unloaded his cargo, containing a wide variety of goods. Carried them well away from his ship and left them. And returned to his ship and waited."

"What happened then?" asked John.

"He fortunately landed on an outlying planet with limited protection. As his ship did not appear to threaten us we held off destroying it. We investigated his goods. We found some that were of interest to us. We then approached his ship. He exited it. We began to make gestures and so did he. You must remember we have a sophisticated trading economy. We indicated what goods we were interested in. He managed to make us understand that we must provide something in return. It took a long time to work out what was most valuable to him, and what the ratio of trade goods was. He seemed to be most interested in gold, and certain biological products. He filled his hold with these, and indicated that he would return to that spot with our most desired trade goods. Which he did, with a larger ship and some human companions. It proved that he was most interested in some of the organics, and a person who you called an exenologist set up a computer system to attempt to learn our language. That is a brief story how trading started at a planet called trrzzfkle two wormholes from this planet. Originally Mr Albrecht controlled the trade, but he soon lost control. Scores of ships landed on this planet, and a large city grew up, where humans and Waps mixed freely. It was only after the collapse in our relations that trade moved here."

"Thank you Fred, that is just about the story I heard. But the Waps were blamed for the collapse of trade and the bad relations," said John.

"We have described our version of events. It was a pity the Humans did not use the intermediation of Mr Albrecht in all this. But he said that they did not trust him."

"Did you remain in contact with Mr Albrecht?" asked John.

"Yes," said Fred, "we maintain regular secret meetings with him at a secret location on the Line. He does his best to help us, and we of course favor him in many things. But we have to keep these contacts secret because he says he would be considered a traitor if it was known."

"Given the limited amount he did to resolve the situation, he was probably using you for his own profit," said John.

"That view might be unjust," said Fred. "He was responsible for setting up the Line and our current trade relations."

"And all those deaths! The sadistic old bastard. Yes I will see him just to tell him that!"

John was waiting in the room alone when an old man walked in from the opposite door, and the door closed.

John rose. "Mr Albrecht I presume," he said.

"Yes," said Johannes Albrecht as he sat down, and he gave a wintery smile, "John Griffin I presume."

Johannes Albrecht was a small bald headed man with small bright eyes. He gave John an intense looking over. "I have heard a lot about you," he said.

"And I have heard something of you," John replied.

"Like what?"

"Well aside from being an evil old bastard, you are supposed to be well over hundred years of age," John said.

Johannes Albrecht smiled, "I am over hundred and forty years old."

"You don't look a day over eighty," John replied.

"Thank you," Albrecht replied, "mainly because I am taking increasing amounts of the life giving drug. Rising at an exponential rate. It delays the loss of telomeres you know."

"I know. I wouldn't use the stuff."

"We'll see, when you get old and rich."

"If….you mean."

"Now enough of this sparring. I came here to see you after I heard your threat to have me strangled."

"I remember you tried to have me killed," John replied.

"That was unfortunate."

"Unfortunate! That was standard company policy! You have an agency problem in your firm. If I was running it, as soon as you had a replacement you could have smuggled us both on a ship," John replied heatedly.

Johannes Albrecht shifted uncomfortably on his chair. "We had other issues with the criminal gang."

"Thanks! At least you admit that it was you that decided to kill both of us. More convenient for you!"

John got up.

"Wait! Wait! I agree. I was slack and remiss. I was overly influenced by my executives. I have realized that, and the firm had what you call an agency problem. I have since tried to remedy that. That callous attitude will not continue in my firm. It got away from me. If it is worth anything to you, I apologize."

"Well, if you think that apology will stop you being garroted if you play up with the cartel, it won't, I have no power in that," John said.

"I understand and I am not here about that. I have given strict instructions to always provide one hundred and five per cent in quality, and if there is a dispute, provide a full restitution without objection."

"Then why are you here?" John asked.

"To see you. Our meeting has confirmed my opinion. We are very similar, you and I. We are very close to the Waps in many respects. And furthermore your handling of the subsequent events and negotiations has gained my respect."

"Even pushing your manager over the Line to get shot?"

Albrecht smiled thinly. "Between you and me, I would have done the same."

John laughed. Albrecht smiled more broadly and they looked into each other's eyes.

"Now listen," Albrecht continued, "I want you to work for me. I can offer you a high paid job as my assistant. Even possibly take over running of the firm."

"The answer is no. But don't you have children, executives, who can do this?"

"None who can gain the respect of the Waps. Fundamentally they all fear them."

John thought for a moment. "You have really offended me by trying to kill me. And what is worse you tried to kill my future wife. Somebody who was totally innocent. What you can do, which will at least get us back into speaking terms, and maybe a willingness to help you in the future, is this. As you have no doubt heard, for the past five years we were hiding on the planet Arieta in the city of Sevilla. We had to flee back here because a large number of people suddenly tried to arrest us. It was a major operation. What I am concerned with is the fate of the people we employed. The lawyer, our compradore, servants, employees. I am sure they suffered and continue to suffer. I want your intervention on their behalf. I want them released. Their complete freedom restored. Their income restored. They should be allowed to go about their lives as if I was still on the planet Arieta. As part of that, it will be necessary to restore sufficient of my property to support them. I am not asking you to restore the ton of gold they have no doubt seized. That is not my primary concern. It is the fate of my servants or friends that is my main concern. If you restore them to the previous status quo I shall be happy to talk to you again."

"That is very commendable of you, I shall see what I can do."

A thought then occurred to John. "However the Waps do not want it confirmed that we were living on Arieta. You will have to keep that a secret."

Johannes Albrecht nodded. He stood up. After a bit of hesitation they shook hands. His hand was dry and leathery. He left through the opposite door.

John thought as he left. "That was most interesting. I hope he fixes the situation on Arieta. And I seem to have fixed the major problems here. I suppose for the next few months I am going to be bored."

CHAPTER EIGHT

The next few days were interspersed with John helping with the negotiations setting up the milk cartel, the arrangements for the milk delivery, "Details, details," thought John; outings to the desert where the kids seemed to show boundless energy and had to be chased everywhere, upsetting the poor Waps driver who just stood waving his arms, "I'll have to double the pay of the nanny if we ever get back to Arieta," he thought. And he was nagged by Gwen, who never seemed happy with the state the children were in.

One night, after getting back happy and exhausted, John fell into bed. "Do you think we are going to be on this planet long?" asked Gwen, climbing into the other side of the bed.

"Another eight months, probably. It will take time. I am working on our return to Arieta. As I told you I have asked Johannes Albrecht to secure the release of our people, and provide them with support. Be patient. You know I fix things in the end," John replied.

"I know," said Gwen, and kissed him, snuggling up to him.

His sleep was interrupted by a dark form above him. "John," it said.

John awakened. "Oh, hello Fred. What is the matter?"

"An event has occurred. It requires your immediate presence."

"What has happened? An interruption in the milk supply?"

"No, something far worse. The human worlds have been attacked. The humans accuse us."

"Are you attacking them?"

"No. We suspect it is the Errrchxz. They must have got past the barrier into your part of space. Found a wormhole. They are now trying to seize planets."

By this time the light was on, Gwen was sitting up, and John was throwing on clothes.

"Why did you not tell us of these enemies?" asked John.

"We did not think it relevant with our relationship with you," said Fred.

"But when we first met you attacked our ships," said John, "was this due to your war with these Erch?"

"Yes, we were in the final phase of a desperate war. These were the only other spacegoing species we knew. We thought that they were coming up behind us," Fred replied.

"How bad are these Erch?" John asked.

"They destroy all sentient beings on the planets the capture. They then breed fast. We have lost many planets to them. We have barely contained them. Indeed we have had to increase our population much faster as a result. That is why we needed your milk. We have found that this liquid improves the survival rate of our offspring. It is vital to us." Fred began to wave his arms and buzz.

"I shall keep the latter information secret for the near future," said John.

He continued, "Fred, I am going to ask you a very important question. What do you think of us humans now?" John asked.

Fred waited a while, then said. "We do not regard you as a threat. If we can solve our differences we can cooperate. We can as you call it like you."

"Fred, you have probably said the most important words in the history of your race. Come on, we will see what we can do!" John said. He gave Gwen a peck on her cheek, and said to Fred, "Where are we going?"

"To the military negotiation center up the line."

They piled into an aircar that did not have padding for humans.

Fred said, "We will be fast." And they were. The aircar rose off the ground to roof height, and screamed at what was at least 600 Kph to the center to the north. They landed. Fred jumped out and said "Come," and ran at full speed into the center. John ran following him.

The center was brightly lit and full. A long line of Waps sitting at a table faced by a long line of people in military uniforms.

A number of humans were talking, or shouting, at once, and the translations did not seem to be coping. There was a buzzing sound from Fred, and one of the Waps slid out of his seat. Some material was shoved onto the seat as padding and John sat down.

There was silence. One of the officers then asked, "Who are you?"

"John Griffin."

"Oh, yes, the traitor."

"Call me what you like, but if you are prepared to listen calmly," and then John turned to another officer who began to shout, "and I said calmly, I have an explanation for all this."

"As if we believe your explanation!" interjected one officer.

"You had better," said John, "otherwise the human worlds are in serious trouble."

"What do you mean?"

"You are being attacked by enemies of the Waps, they call the Erch. I have not got full details, but when they capture a planet they wipe out all sentient beings, breed fast, and take over more planets. Is this so, Fred?"

"Yes, that is correct. We have fought them a long time and they have taken over many of our planets, killing our people. We have fought them to a standstill. But it appears they have found a wormhole through the rift and are finding new planets to conquer."

There was silence.

"You claim it is not you?" one asked.

"No, we are not attacking the humans," replied Fred.

Another silence.

"May I make a suggestion here?" asked John.

"What is it?" said the chief officer.

"Probably there have already been clashes. Even planets under attack. There will be wreckage and casualties on their side. I suggest that you inspect the debris, and see what form your attackers take. If they are not Waps, you know it is not them. The Waps can provide images of these Erch, which is what they call them, for comparison."

There was silence.

Then one officer asked antagonistically, "And what if they are allies of the Waps?"

John drew a breath, and looked at the Waps. "I have only one suggestion to make. If the Waps can spare a squadron or fleet, and you can spare a similar fleet, both of you together can attack these Erch. This will prove that you are on the same side."

"And if they are not?"

"You will lose a fleet, but know definitely you are fighting a war on two fronts."

"Would the Waps be willing to do this?"

"I don't know," replied John, "They will have to consider it. So will you. As times are desperate, I suggest a break for no longer than an hour. We will return with our decisions." John got up, turned and walked away.

After a hesitation, the humans and the Waps did the same.

After they had left the building Fred asked, "What do you think will be their decision?"

"They will what we call temporize. They will need more time. They cannot make an immediate decision on such an alliance, a joint battle fleet. They must refer it to the home government to make such a decision, and indeed they won't make such a decision unless they are really pressed. But first, they will not be so angry and blaming you. They will ask for more information, such as the appearance of the Erch. In the next hour you must prepare visuals of the Erch, their ships, and if possible their effects on the planets they capture. We can supply that information along the cable we laid through the building just before I left last time. Also, this is important, I will call what is called a press conference after the next meeting is finished, explaining the attack was not by the Waps, but by these Erch, and supplying the visuals you supplied the military. Can you do that? I know it is a lot to do?"

Fred said "Certainly. You are not asking for an immediate decision on a Waps-Human alliance?"

"No. Just sound positive. I don't know what your decision making process is, but if you think it is a good idea, you can enter negotiations with then when their government decides to negotiate, and agree to an alliance. It will take time. I suspect that when they get pressed, it will all happen in a rush."

Fred again appeared to chuckle. "As I said before, you are invaluable to us."

"Fred, I am doing this to help both sides. Not for your credit. I would be happy to get out of this just a trip back to Arieta."

"We will drop you on the mountain again."

"No. I want to return in full view, and live there with my wife and children legally and peacefully."

Fred again chuckled. "We will see what we can do."

"In the meantime Fred," John said, "I have had no breakfast. Within the next hour, can you return me to the apartment to something to eat, check on the family, and return me?"

John and the Waps re-entered the building first, and soon the officers came in at sat down.

John immediately announced, "The Waps have prepared images of the Erch. They can send them over the cable if you can receive them."

"Yes, we are ready," said the presiding officer.

"OK, Fred, transmit," John said.

Fred replied, "Images transmitted."

The officer commenced, "We have received reports that creatures have landed on planets and have begun massacring the inhabitants. They will not allow surrender. Our ships are having difficulty containing them."

"Is the military talk that their ships are superior?" John asked.

The officer looked uncomfortable, "That is not necessarily so…"

"It looks as if this situation is a lot more serious than I originally thought. Transmit our offer to Earth immediately. Would the Waps be willing to consider an alliance with the humans to defeat the Waps?" He turned to Fred.

"Yes," Fred answered without hesitation.

"An alliance?"

"Yes. We can discuss details, but the situation is a lot more serious than you realize. If the Erch, as John has named them, manage to establish on many planets, they will seriously threaten us. They must be contained, and if possible destroyed. And we must start now. Delay will make events worse."

The presiding officer coughed and squirmed on his seat. "We will have to discuss this with our government."

"John has explained that," said Fred, "but please explain to your government that the situation is extremely dangerous and delays will make things worse. We are willing to move at any time."

"Right, we will consider this. Just as a matter of interest how many ships can you throw into this?"

"We have over two hundred ships waiting on the other side of the immediate wormhole."

John thought, "That's upset them."

But Fred remorsessly continued, “How long will it take to obtain a decision from you home government?”

“I don’t know,” replied the officer, “If they are agreeable, at least a month.”

“That is too long,” said Fred.

“Well….that is the best we can do,” replied the officer.

“We will immediately send a fleet through alternative wormholes. You will supply us with the current locations of the Erch. You will inform your fleets not to fire on us.”

The officers mouth opened. “But…but….yyou can’t do that! It is our space!”

“Note any more,” said Fred. “The Erch must be destroyed. We will return to our space if we do that.”

John said in the dead silence following. “It is wise to cooperate. The Waps are trying to help you. Please supply them with what information you have.”

The officer looked at his colleagues. “We will consider…”

“Now. I am informing the press. By this evening.”

The officers looked dumbfounded and hurriedly left.

The press conference was chaotic. John had demanded the use of the Court on the line, and specified a start on the ninth hour.

At exactly the hour John yelled "Silence!"

People were still drifting in, and John asked Fred, "Is there any way of amplifying my voice?"

Fred said "Yes. Use this," and he attached a device to John's chest. "Double my volume."

"Silence," yelled John. Immediately there was an ear splitting roar.

"I will now speak in my normal voice. Those who don't like it remain outside."

"I shall start by telling you that human kind is at war. Shhh!" He raised his hands. "Not with the Waps, but with the creatures call the Erch. E-R-C-H."

"The Waps will supply visuals of the Erch, the same visuals which the Waps have supplied to the military. Please transmit, Fred."

"Done."

"The Erch have entered human space through wormholes unknown to the humans, and are attacking human planets."

There were a lot of yells and questions.

"I will answer questions later."

"These Erch, so the Waps tell us, after they land on a planet, kill all sentient beings on the planet, breed fast, and then proceed to take over more planets."

The noise fell to near silence.

"The Waps have been fighting them for a long time, and have managed to contain them. They are enemies of the Waps."

"The Waps propose an alliance. They will move into human space and attack these Erch. Hopefully with the assistance of human ships."

There was a collective intake of breath.

"The Waps say that there is no time for delay. Any delay makes the Erch stronger. The Waps intend to attack the Erch now."

John waited in the anticipatory silence.

"The Waps fleet intends to proceed through other wormholes they know into human space and attack the Erch immediately."

There was a low mumble.

"The Waps realize that there has been little notice or warning. They request that the human fleets engaging the Erch be warned to expect the Waps fleet and not fire on them. They must be warned that the Waps fleet is coming to assist."

"Negotiations for an alliance will proceed concurrently with the assistance the Waps are providing to the human fleet."

Any questions?

"What do the Erch look like?"

"Visuals have been provided. Next question."

"How long have the Waps been fighting the Erch?"

"Fred?"

"Two hundred years before contact with the humans. We have lost nearly one hundred planets. We have not managed to regain any. We are still fighting them to contain their expansion."

"Why do the Erch want to capture planets?"

"Food and resources mainly. When they have eaten all the creatures they can, they begin to cultivate the entire surface, and start manufacturing their war machines," said Fred.

"Do you mean they eat Waps?"

"Yes, they eat all the Waps on the planet. Then all creatures above a very small size."

"Everything?"

"Yes."

John interceded. "And just to make the point clear they will eat all the humans on the planets they capture."

There were shouts of "I don't believe it!" and "Nonsense!".

"I suppose you know the Erch," John said. "If we manage to recapture any of these planets, you will find out."

Then John raised his hands. "Now listen. I want the Waps to be provided with the locations of where these attacks are taking place. By this evening. I have requested this information from the military."

He stood up to go. He received one last question. "Why have the Waps set up a milk supply cartel for just four firms?"

John laughed. "You are about to be eaten alive and you worry about a milk supply cartel!" He turned and left the room.

"We have a lot to do," John said to Fred, "What is your first priority?"

"We need to know where the attacks are occurring," said Fred.

"Even if the humans told you, how would you understand the exact location from the human coordinates they give you?"

"Even a general location would be useful. We must start immediately," replied Fred.

"I will get you this information and devices which will assist you with the exact location," said John.

Fred clicked his fingers. "Do you have influence with the military?"

"No, but I have influence with someone who can supply this information immediately and supply the devices today – Johannes Albrecht."

He rang the headquarters of Albrecht and Company in Port City.

"My name is John Griffin. Put me through to Johannes Albrecht immediately. You have no doubt been instructed to do so," John said.

After a short delay he faced Johannes Albrecht on the screen. "Johannes, you have heard of today's events. I want you to do some things for me immediately."

Albrecht raised his eyebrows. "No please?"

"Pleeeeze. It is your leathery skin which is going to get eaten."

Albrecht smiled. "What do you want?"

"The Waps fleet intends to take off this evening and attack the Erch in human space. To do this they need the exact location of these attacks. You must immediately obtain this information from the military, every last detail they know, and supply it to us. Fred, the Waps, is your contact. Send this information though your usual channels. That's first." Albrecht's eyes shifted to the others in the room. "Second," continued John remorselessly, "you will supply navigation equipment which contain all the galactic coordinates of known human space. You will supply as many of these devices as possible. Today. They must reach the Waps by this evening. I know it is several thousand kilometers so you must load the equipment on a fast air car and break the speed of sound to bring this equipment to the line on time. To your main selling location on the Line. Where I worked. The Waps will not shoot it down. Will you, Fred?"

"No, we will be aware what the vehicle is and not shoot it down," answered Fred.

"Next, you will supply an expert to quickly instruct the Waps how to use the navigation equipment. And oh yes, if this equipment needs power, you must supply equipment to convert the power on the Waps' spaceships to the needs of these machines. Fred is your contact on the technical details."

"Is that all," Albrecht asked sardonically.

"You provide the name and number of a competent contact person. Instruct him to respond immediately to the Waps requests, and supply their requests immediately," answered John.

"You heard that Frank, you're it," said Albrecht to someone off the screen.

"You don't mean this?" answered the voice of the screen.

"Yes, if the Waps say it is serious, it is serious. What is your number?" Albrecht asked Frank. He supplied the number to John and asked, "Anything else?"

"I can't think of anything else at the moment. I am already stressed out," replied John.

"Will do. Best of luck." Albrecht waited and looked at him. "I presume you are going to join their fleet."

"I have not discussed it with them yet. But yes, it is logical and if they need me I will."

Albrecht moved his cheeks. "I have heard of these battles with the Erch. Few survive. I wish you well." He looked sadly at John.

Fred hummed. "As he says, the conflicts are extremely dangerous. The Erch constantly learn, and their vessels are nearly the equal of our own."

John replied. "You will be contacting humans, and attempting to fight with them. You will need a person to contact them and discuss with them. This will increase your chances of winning."

"I agree," said Fred, "but you have a mate and children. What I have seen of humans there is a close emotional bond."

"That is true," answered John, "but throughout human history this has happened. Women and children grieve when their men go to war. But they are used to it. It is normal behavior for humans. They hope their men return."

"We will happy to have you on board our ships to assist us," said Fred.

"Fred, I shall need sufficient human food in those self heating packs and bars to last me," said John. "Now what are the toilet facilities like?"

"They will be very limited," said Fred. "That is of concern to us, and is indeed the main reason why we did not immediately ask you to join us. There will be no shower."

John laughed. "Forget the shower. I will arrange to obtain a chemical toilet. This should cope for hopefully a few months if we get sufficient supplies for it."

Fred asked, "Shall I ask this man Frank for one?"

"No, since it is vital, I had better cross the Line to obtain one myself. Inform Frank that I will cross the Line at the trade station to make purchases in one hour. Tell him that they should have an armed guard and a vehicle waiting for me, to escort me there and back."

"Yes, John."

"I shall in the meantime return to my apartment to ask my wife to pack."

"Will this cause an emotional response?" asked Fred.

"Yes, it will. But she will understand."

As soon as he requested Gwen that she pack all his clothes, she realized what was happening, and collapsed weeping. It took a best part of an hour for John to calm her. "Oh, John!" she finally said. "You must come back to me and our children! I love you. The children too."

"Yes, darling, I shall return. But I must hurry off to do a few things. I will be back this afternoon to pick up my clothes." He hurried out.

At the trade station, John crossed the Line, to be met by a group of grim faced security people. "Hi fellers," he said as he walked past them and into the vehicle. "I presume we won't have any problem with the police or anyone else?"

"No, they have been warned," was the grim replay.

At the camping store John purchased the chemical toilet, a large quantity of chemicals, and two lightweight sleeping bags with floor pads. He was already thinking ahead. They then quickly returned to the trade station, and re-crossed the Line with his purchases.

The conflict location information was quickly sent to the Waps, and later in the afternoon a large high-speed air car screamed in to drop down in front of the trade station. John met them. The equipment was taken out of the car and taken over the Line. They were accompanied by a man. He hesitated when he reached the Line. “Don’t worry,” said John, “no harm will come to you.” The man stepped over.

“Now,” said John, ”this equipment needs to be installed in our ships, and you must instruct the Waps how to use it. You have another trip ahead of you. Get in this air car, and we will get there quickly.”

“Oh, oh!” said the man, “What am I getting in to!”

“Don’t worry, after you have installed the equipment and instructed the Waps, you will be returned here safe and sound.”

As soon as they got into the car, he noticed a pile of clothes in the passenger apartment.

John saw his glance. “I am going with the Waps,” he said. He tried to forget the heart wrenching parting with Gwen, who had seized him and covered his shirt with tears. But everything he needed was there.

The air car screamed to the port, and landed as the sun was going down. There was one obvious military vessel on the ground, and a lot of scurrying round it. They got out of the car under the shadow of the setting sun. There was a deputation of Waps waiting including Fred.

“Before we start, “ announced John, “we had better check that all these devices work with the

Waps military electric power. Just connect them up, turn them on and see if they work."

This took a best part of an hour, with leads leading everywhere as they connected the devices up and switched them on. Soon half a dozen pieces of equipment were glowing in the dark.

"Now," said John, "next step. Oh what's your name?" he asked the man.

"Norman," he replied, "but call me Norm."

"Well, Norm, insert these locations provided us of the conflict into the machines, carefully demonstrating to the Waps how it is done."

Norm did so, but it took a while for the group of what were Waps specialist navigators to understand the working of the equipment. It was not helped that some of the devices varied and had different controls. There was not full comprehension even by midnight.

"You have to do this to rotate the image," said Norm for the umpteenth time.

"Norm, a horrible thought has occurred to me," said John. "The Waps do not perceive 3-D screens as we do. 2-D are ok, but 3-D is a lot more difficult. These things are not going to work without a human operator."

"You will be going," said Norm.

"Yup, but I am not an expert."

There was a pregnant silence.

"You want me to come?"

"We need you to come," replied John.

Norm looked around. "I was not told about this."

"We did not expect it."

Norm glanced around. John continued, "You will be helping the survival of the human race. And the Waps will be very grateful."

"Yeah, how grateful?"

"They can get very grateful. Pay in thousands of kilos of gold."

Fred took up the cue. "If you assist us, we will pay you one thousand kilos of gold."

Norm licked his lips. "Instant millionaire. OK, you have convinced me. I'll go." He turned to Fred, "Me, navigator."

"You do not need to communicate in such simple language. But, welcome aboard." And he held out one of his hands, which Norm shook with a surprised look on his face.

"Well, get all this equipment aboard," shouted John.

John looked at Fred. "Are you coming too?"

"Yes. It is necessary. You need someone to look after you. I will be your minder."

"Well, thanks, Fred. But your language seems to be changing."

"I have watched many human films to try to understand human behavior. I hope I am using the correct nomenclature."

"A bit old fashioned, but it is OK."

"I have watched many twentieth century films to try to understand your relationships and behavior."

"Oh, right, and which is your favorite film?"

"I found the films of battles on the surface of your seas interesting. But they did not have many female relationships. I found most interesting a film where the men leave their girls behind them and sing before riding into battle. This singing I find strange. Do you always sing before going into battle?"

"Only in films," John said dryly.

Eventually Fred showed them to a cabin. "I am sorry it does not have a shower," said Fred. John sighed in exasperation. "Why do the Waps keep saying this?" he thought. It was very small, with John's clothes stacked on one side, the chemical toilet installed at one end, and a basin.

"We will sleep on each side of the loo," said John, "we will divide the clothes between us. I hope you will be comfortable."

"This is going to be fun," said Norm.

CHAPTER NINE

John pulled out the sleeping bags and mats, and gave one each to Norm. "I see. You expected me to come."

"I made preparations just in case," said John. "Now I am going to take a kip. I suggest that you do too. I have been up nearly twenty-four hours, and I am exhausted. Oh yeah, I had better fix up the loo. Where are the chemicals?" But the Waps had already done it. They had read the instructions and inserted the correct dose of chemicals. "I can rely on them if they know what to do," thought John. He used the loo to test if it worked. Then said, "All yours. I am crashing." Laid out in sleeping bag, and was asleep in seconds.

He woke somewhat groggy. Norm was already awake and drinking some water from the tap on the basin, with a lot of snorting and crashing. John struggled up, said "Hi, slept well?" And also drank some water from the tap..

"Well, we had better sort out what we have got," John said. "Then we can talk."

Norm said, "This place is like a prison."

"Don't worry, as soon as the Waps know we are up and about, they will keep us plenty busy. OK, the clothing and underwear, half goes to you. You can choose what you want. We can have equal piles. I suggest put them down next to the loo."

John found that Gwen had shoved in two tooth-brushes, paste, and other washing needs including towels, a book reader and there was a letter. He opened it. It read:

"My Darling John, I have packed all your clean clothes and anything else I can think of. I hope you will be comfortable on that ship. I am sure the Waps will look after you. Fred says he will go with you, and another Waps will be assigned to look after me. I will miss Fred. The children will miss you and are very upset. Hugh and Emma send their love. They say you are very brave. I know you are. Come back to me, my darling. I love you passionately. I will miss you greatly. Lots of love and kisses, Gwen. P.S. Look after yourself!!! Don't do anything silly!!" The letter was covered in tear-stains.

John carefully folded the letter, and put it in his shirt pocket. There were tears in his eyes.

They divided up the pile of clothes and the washing things. The sat down with their backs to the wall facing each other and began to talk.

"Well, I suppose I had better ask if you have been in a space ship before?" asked John.

"I was Johannes Albrecht's personal pilot," Norm replied. He looked in his late thirties with short brown hair with specks of white, and a creased face, but it was difficult to tell what age he was. There seemed to be a lot of experience behind his eyes.

"Are you married? Children?"

"No. I am from a planet that imposes a financial requirement for marriage and children. I was in the Space Navy. A pilot. I got out and was offered a good job. Basically shuttling Johannes Albrecht and some of his executives between Earth and The Line."

" A cushy job," said John.

"I was saving to get married. A girl I know."

"Well, if you get back in one piece you certainly will be able to get married."

"Huh."

"Don't blame Albrecht. He had a pretty good idea that the Waps will compensate you well if you survive."

"Will they," said Norm hopefully.

"Well, for what were relatively minor services from my point of view they paid me three thousand kilos. Save their bacon, pal, and the minimum you will get is one thousand kilos. They are wholly honest and rational. They estimate what they owe you from their point of view…"

At this point the door slid open, and Fred stood there. "I see that you have rested. We have gone through three wormholes and we are approaching the fleet."

"What can we do to help?" asked John.

"While we have set up one of your machines, the output is still incomprehensible," replied Fred.

John got up. "Lets have a look." Norm struggled to his feet also.

They were led down a set of narrow corridors, squeezing past Waps coming the other way, and up circular stairs until they reached what looked like a bridge. Norm looked around and seemed to understand what was happening.

"Fred," said John, "While I have been sleeping I have been thinking about your problem."

"I am glad to hear that. You already have a solution?"

"Possibly. You remember when we connected up computers across the Line at the Courthouse to facilitate the transfer of data for the accounting process?" John asked.

"Yes, I do. I remember the process was a success," replied Fred.

"Yes, the initial problem was that while the human computers operated on eight bit words, Waps computers operate on twelve bit words."

"Yes. The explanation is because we have twelve fingers, three on each hand."

"Whatever. Anyway the technicians very quickly set it up so that the Waps and Human computers talked to each other."

"That is true. Now these machines are specialized computers. How can our computers talk to them?"

John continued. "Now as Norm is familiar with these devices he can show you the port which connects to the memory of these computers. As I am sure your people have a record of what you did previously, you can get the machines talking."

"John, you are invaluable!" said Fred.

"I have a further suggestion. As we have several of these machines, we can set them up in other suitable ships. The reason is that even if we get access, I doubt if the process will be that simple. You might ruin the memories of a couple. But as we have five of them, I am sure one ship will be successful, and they will be able to extract the information they need direct from the machine's memory and convert it into something useful."

"John, you are beyond price if this works!" said Fred waving his arms.

"Well, we had better get started. I shall help Norm."

Pretty soon they worked out how to connect up the ports, while the Waps dug up the information on the connection process on the Line. There was a lot of humming among the Waps technicians. "There are a lot of difficulties," said Fred, "there are a lot of prohibitions and encryption in the data." Then suddenly the machine froze, there was a crackling sound, and smoke came out of it.

"One down, four more to go!" announced John. "Norm, grab one of a different make. This time a cheap consumer brand. All we need is what is in the memory."

Norm connected it up, and just at that moment there was sudden activity on the bridge. Fred announced, "We have reached the fleet."

"Well, Fred, arrange a shuttle to take the other three machines to the fleet. One of these four will work."

After a while, and a lot of activity, Fred announced, "We have placed the three other machines in a small vessel. What you call a packet boat." He seemed to be enjoying himself. "We will proceed to deliver them and set them up."

They got into a vessel slightly larger than the one that had delivered him to the surface of Arieta. The couches were padded. "Strap yourself in!" said Fred. With a jerk they were flung out into space. There was a high acceleration, then maneuvering and decelerating. There was a bang, and they stopped.

Fred said "Detach restraints." The door opened and they were on the deck of another ship. "This is what you call a flagship. It is equivalent to what you call a seventy-four."

John rolled his eyes and thought, "I hope he is not going to keep up these funny remarks dredged from old films. I preferred the old didactic Fred."

One of the machines had already been taken out and was place on the back of a vehicle. "Step in, make yourself comfortable and hold tight," announced Fred.

The vehicle started and headed down wide lighted corridors at high speed, avoiding vehicles coming the other way. They shot through a sliding door, slowed and stopped. They were in a large room surrounded by flashing monitors.

Waps detached the machine and set it down near what were obviously computers. There was a Waps waiting for them wearing some sort of insignia. There was some humming between them.

Fred announced, "The Admiral welcomes you to his flagship. He is grateful that you have come so far."

"Greetings to the Admiral," replied John, "and thank him for his kind words. With his permission we will connect his computer to our machine. Be warned the machine will resist having its mind read. The humans put these resistances in to prevent them stealing each others' data."

There was further humming. Fred said, "Have no fear. Now that you have warned us, we will be very careful."

Norm quickly attached the cables, which had obviously been prepared on the instruction of the other ship. There was a lot of humming among the Waps, and flashing lights. The Fred said, "We have analyzed the encryption and we are working on the traps. The technicians will be careful."

"Well, Norm, we had better go. Next ship." He turned to the admiral. "Greetings Admiral. I hope you are successful against the Erch." The Admiral bowed slightly, waved one of his hands and hummed. Fred said, "He says we are very grateful for your assistance. He also says that he would have liked to have you both transferred to his ship. However they do not have the time and resources at the present time, as they are in a hurry. He will place the ship you are in part of the fleet which is of lower risk."

The next three ships, while not quite as big as the flagship, were also really massive. "I don't know what they are compared to ours, but they are impressive," said John. In each the Waps quickly connected up the machines and began working on them. They had obviously had been forewarned.

When they got back to their own ship, John asked Norm, "Well what do you think of that?"

"I would not like to come up against these. I don't know what their armaments are, but my guess they would make short work of anything human."

When they reached the cabin, Fred announced, "I have just been told that one of the lesser ships has cracked it. Is that the right expression?"

"Yes, Fred. That is good news. You now know everything on human space. I hope this was not an elaborate ruse. I trusted you."

Fred hummed and waved all four limbs. "I assure you that the threat from the Erch is true. We only seek friendship with the humans."

"That's good," sighed John. "Maybe there is something you can do for me. I am concerned for the safety of my home world Arieta. It is up near the rift and those worm holes across it. If it is convenient for you, can you ascertain from the information provided whether they are in any danger, please?"

"I will do my best, John."

"Well, we shall have a rest and a meal in our cozy little cabin," said John. He collapsed on his sleeping bag.

CHAPTER TEN

They were woken up by an almighty bang. Gravity seemed to quiver and they were picked up and thrown against the wall. Before reaching it they were frozen in absolute stasis, before after a while drifting slowly down back to the floor. Lights flickered.

"We are under attack," said Norm in a low voice.

There were strange noises coming down the corridor, and the cabin began to warm up. John realized that the ventilation had been cut off.

Then slowly things returned to normal. The ventilation returned, the light stopped flickering, and gravity returned to normal.

After a while the door slid back and Fred appeared. He seemed to be a bit singed.

"What is your status?" he asked. His translator did not seem to be working properly.

"We are fine. No injuries," replied John.

"Good. We would have been sorry to lose you," replied Fred. He waited as his translator seemed to get into gear. "We have had a fight with the Erch. We have won this contact. The Erch fleet was largely destroyed. A small number fled. Our casualties are small, but we have lost our flag ship."

"I am sorry to hear that," replied John.

"I am too. We trapped the Erch. We surprised them. They were pursuing a human fleet. We came up behind them." Fred waited. "We now need to talk to the human fleet."

"I am at your service," said John.

"Ah, like Rhett Butler," said Fred.

"Something like that," said John.

Fred took him to the bridge. It was in chaos, and smoke lay heavily in the air. As far as John could ascertain, there was a new captain.

"We are travelling in parallel to the human fleet. They have now tried to contact us," said Fred.

"I shall talk to them," said John.

"Hello, please identify yourself." A voice kept repeating over the loudspeaker.

"What do you want me to say?" asked John.

"Gain their confidence. Tell them we are allies. Then ask them to take a place to the rear of our fleet," said the captain.

"Yes, line astern," said Fred.

"We intend to go through the next wormhole. We know an Erch fleet will be waiting there. That is their usual tactic. They chase a fleet into their trap," continued the captain.

"What is the system up ahead?" asked John.

"It is the system of Arieta."

John's heart froze.

"If you can, you must get the human fleet to block that worm hole so the Erch do not escape through it. We will engage the enemy and if possible block the other two worm holes in the system. That way the Erch will be destroyed," he continued.

"Yes, the humans must head them off at the gulch," said Fred, waving a couple of hands.

"I will have to tell Fred these film references are not appropriate," thought John. "I suppose he thinks he is being more human."

"Put them on" said John.

"Hello, this is the accompanying fleet. Over an out," said John.

Norm said, "Forget the over and out business. They will just respond."

After a wait, a voice asked "Who is that?"

"This is John Griffin, the liaison officer for the fleet which destroyed the ships that you are fighting. We are your allies."

"Allies? Who are you?"

"We are a Waps fleet. The fleet that attacked you was the Erch. They are enemies of the Waps."

"We did not know the Waps were our allies."

"The Earth government will soon inform you. Just understand that the Waps saved you."

"Are you human?" the voice asked.

"Yes I am human," replied John, "and I have a human Naval officer with me." John turned and whispered "Give them your full Naval rank, the lot."

Norm bent over and said, "This is Commander Norman Foster, of the Fifth Fleet, based at Arzac. For you information my serial number is JZA675621."

There was a wait.

"Commander, you are on the Reserve list," said the voice.

"Well I am back on active service as Liaison Officer."

"Well, we are sure glad to see you. We were in big trouble."

There was a wait.

There was a change in voice. "Can we see you guys in person?"

"Can't you come to our ship?" John asked.

"We prefer not to," was the terse reply.

John looked at Fred. "Yes, that can be arranged, though we will be sorry to lose you if anything happens to you," Fred replied.

"I shall return, Fred, I promise. But we have no space suits," said John.

"We have a very small vessel, which may be able to enter the human vessel."

"We are discussing your request," said John, returning to the speaking apparatus. "We have no space suits. We have a small vessel. Can it enter yours?"

"What size is it?"

There was a humming sound. "Twelve meters long, and four meters in diameter."

"It can enter a port nose first and then must back out when leaving," said the speaker.

More humming among the Waps. "Yes, that is satisfactory," said the Waps Captain. "Leave the port open and brightly lit. Then bang on the side when air pressure has been adjusted."

There were four of them in the tiny craft. The pilot and Fred in the front seats of the tiny craft, John and Norm in the rear. The hatch was closed with a click, they heard pumps and the sound fell to zero, the port opened and they slid out. They approached the human fleet. The largest ship had a port open which was brightly lit, and the pilot adjusted speed and carefully slid into it. The heard a thump as the door closed, and the sound of air. Then they heard banging on the side.

The pilot slowly opened the hatch, and John and Norm saw humans staring in.

"Come with us please," said a Petty Officer. They climbed out and John said, "We have a companion." Fred climbed out and the humans stared and stepped back.

"He's harmless," said John. "He is a representative of the fleet out there. Take us to your commanding officer."

They were escorted up corridors past staring personnel, to a cabin containing a number of officers. "I am Commodore Jackson," said one of the men standing there. "I am John Griffin," said John. "And I am Commander Foster," said Norm, and he continued, "And this is the Waps liaison officer. You may address him as Fred."

"I am delighted to meet you," said Fred.

"Well," said the Commodore, "I must thank you for destroying the pursuing fleet."

"We are glad to be of service," said Fred.

"You say the pursuing fleet are your enemies," said the Commodore.

"Yes," Fred replied, "we have been fighting the Erch for over two hundred of your years. When we learnt that they had managed to penetrate human space we had no option but to pursue them."

"Yes," said John, "The Erch take over planets, eat all the inhabitants, use all the resources of that planet to build more war fleets and continue their conquests."

"You are joking!"

"Have you managed to contact any inhabitants of planets already conquered?"

"Not after the first few weeks. And the First Fleet was decimated. We are all that is left."

"I have worse news for you. The Erch was chasing you into a trap. Through the wormhole ahead was another Erch fleet. I am told that is a usual tactic."

There was silence.

"Now," said John, "I do not intend to offend anyone's pride, but it should be clear to all of you that your ships are no match for the ships of the Erch. What we want you to do is to attach yourself to the tail of the Waps fleet. The Waps will burst through the wormhole and take the Erch by surprise. Hopefully they will be able to destroy nearly all of their ships."

John continued, “You do have a role to play, though it will be a dangerous one.” There was a slight stir among the officers. “You need to block the wormhole you will exit through into the Arieta system, and stop the Erch escaping back though it. The Waps will block the other two wormholes in the Arieta system, and hopefully prevent Erch escaping further into human space. Your ships will be the last to go through the wormhole, and you must take a station at the other side.”

He turned to Norman. “Commander, have I described the situation correctly?”

“Yes. But we have no appreciation of Erch strength,” he answered.

“Fred, is this what the Waps want?’

“Yes, the Erch must be made to run the gauntlet if they wish to go back through the wormhole.”

“But the Waps will be doing their damndist to see that few if any Erch ships reach you,” John said quickly.

“Alternatively you can follow our tail in and try to stay out of trouble. You cannot return the way you have come as Erch will be waiting for you,” John said.

The Commodore and his men looked very uncomfortable.

“I shall discuss it with our commanders and let you know,” he said.

“When are we entering the wormhole?” John asked Fred.

"Two hours."

"At the very least stay out of our way and attached to our tail," John said to the Commodore.

"Well, now, do you fellers want a drink?" asked the Commodore.

"I can't stay more than a couple of minutes, but I am desperate for a drink. A gin and tonic if you have one." "A Scotch," said Norman.

"Splice the mainbrace!" said Fred.

"Fred!" said John, "these references from old films, while I am sure they are well meant, are out of context. Please revert to your old self."

"I thought that they would make you happy."

"They do, but they are not appropriate for meetings like this."

"I apologise. I shall confine these remarks to private conversation."

After saying farewell to the human officers, they returned to their ship.

When they reappeared on the bridge the captain announced, "The human fleet is taking up station on our rear."

CHAPTER ELEVEN

Back in their cabin, Norm instructed John to put on some head covering. "I don't know what the Waps use, but you may have noticed human battle crews wear helmets and strap down. Stuff pants with clothing and stick them on your head, and tie them on with a shirt. You don't want your head splattered against the ceiling."

"I hope their stasis thing works," replied John, but he put on the ridiculous head-gear. They then sat down opposite each other side-by-side and waited with their backs to opposite walls, and feet braced against the other wall.

"I wonder what damage this ship sustained," asked John.

"I took a glance out of the port of the shuttle. The rear third of the top of the ship has been melted."

"Nasty. Do humans have those weapons?"

"Nope."

About forty minutes later they felt the jump through a wormhole. Almost immediately they felt tremendous power pulsating through the ship. Suddenly they began to lift from the floor, followed immediately by stasis. They looked in each other's eyes. The stasis seemed to hold for quite a long time, before they were slowly lowered back to the floor.

"Well…." said John, but there was as sudden movement in the opposite direction and they were gripped by stasis again. This time they heard a roaring and pounding sound. They were gradually released. Norm licked his lips. He had a hunted look in his eyes. "God, I want to go to the toilet! Oh, there it goes," he moaned as his pants become wet around his crotch and water began to spread around him. "He obviously knows more of what is going on than I do," thought John. There was thud, not as bad as the previous bang, and the light flickered. Then stasis again and another roaring sound.

After that things settled down. The ship occasionally fired, as that was what the rumbling sound clearly was, but there were no longer any occasions of stasis, and finally even these sounds died down.

John asked Norm, "Do you think the battle is over?"

"Yes, from my experience space battles are over pretty quickly. One side rapidly overcomes the other, and the losing side runs for it."

"Back through the wormhole. I hope the First Fleet did not get mauled."

"We shall see."

Norm subsided into silence, staring into the distance. He was obviously carrying some baggage on this. Maybe he was older than what John originally estimated.

Finally the door slid open. "Are you both well?" he asked.

"Yes, we are well," said John without elaboration.

"Do you wear objects on your head for battle?" asked Fred.

"No, to protect our heads. They are delicate if they strike the wall with force, and we can be killed," replied John, struggling from the floor.

"Oh, I am sorry," replied Fred.

"Norm tells me human naval personnel wear helmets, head protection, when going into battle."

"Oh, I am sorry. I should have thought of that. I have seen humans wear helmets in films," said Fred, projecting some degree of concern into his voice.

"Maybe we can borrowed couple of helmets from the human fleet," suggested John.

"When they approach the planet we can request them," said Fred.

"I take it then we were successful?" asked John.

"Yes, we destroyed the Erch fleet. Two escaped through the wormhole. The humans destroyed four, more than we expected. They lost one of their own ships unfortunately. We lost one in five of our ships, which is a better ratio than usual for these clashes. Yes, we were successful."

"I am very glad to hear that. Now what do you want us to do?"

"We need to communicate with both the human fleet, and the planet. Please come to the bridge," said Fred.

"Can I stay behind to clean up?" asked Norm.

"Yes. You are not immediately needed. When you wish to join us open the door and communicate with a member of the crew," answered Fred.

"How do I open the door?"

"Oh, I am sorry. Just place your hand on this patch. The door will open," answered Fred.

John was taken to the Bridge. "First put me through to the Fleet," said John.

"I will open communication. You must speak," said a Waps.

"Hello, First Fleet. This is John Griffin. Please answer."

There was a long wait. The Waps Captain said, "While we left subspace communicators behind, there will be still be a delay to communicate with the fleet."

"I understand."

"Hello, this is Commodore Jackson."

"Congratulations on destroying four Erch ships," said John into the speaker.

"We lost one of our own," said voice.

"I am very sorry to hear that."

"Is it all over now?"

"According to the Waps, the Erch fleet has been completely destroyed."

"I am glad to hear that. What do you want us to do now?"

John looked at the Captain. “What do you request?” he asked.

“We would like them to guard the wormhole, unless the commander feels he can be of some assistance to the planet. The Erch have landed.”

The voice from the speaker said, “I heard that. What is the situation on the ground?”

“The Erch have partly taken over the southern continent.” John’s guts constricted. “Some fighting is happening but of course it is inadequate. However the Erch forces will not now be reinforced.”

“I have one hundred Marines. Will they be of any use,” the Commodore asked over the speaker.

John blurted, “Yes, please! It will be a tremendous morale boost. So will be the arrival of the Earth fleet!”

“What’s left of us.”

“Commodore, I will, with The Waps permission, give you full credit for rescuing their planet. I will also tell them you will land Marines,” John said.

The Commodore chuckled. “Well, we will stick around until we get orders form Earth.”

They then communicated with the planet Arieta. The original communication was in Standard, but John quickly switched to Spanish.

“Hello. The enemy fleet has been completely destroyed. The First Fleet will be in orbit around Arieta shortly. They will land Space Marines on the southern continent to assist your defence.”

There voice replied, "Senor! I am overjoyed! To be rescued by the fleet! We were praying for rescue. We sent to Earth pleading for help. We have been saved!" There was cheering and hubbub in the background.

"Warn Sevilla that Space Marines will be landing shortly."

"Si, Senor, si. How many….?"

"I will be in contact again shortly, over and out."

"Well," said John, "that should keep them going for a while."

They orbited Arieta while the human flagship came in and sent the Marines down to the surface. The Commodore came on to the transmitter and announced that he had been invited down to the capital, Merida.

"That's fine with us," John told him, "The Waps fleet is about to depart. We shall be leaving the welfare of the planet in your hands. Can you do something for me please?"

"What's that?"

"I am a resident of Arieta. Of the city of Sevilla, on the southern continent. I am well known there as José Fernandez, though I am also known there as Senor Peter Brown. I had to leave there suddenly a couple of months ago. If you go to Sevilla, just tell them all that I shall return soon. Many thanks."

"I shall tell them that, I shall also tell them that their deliverance is due to your Waps."

"Not my Waps. Just the Waps I am assisting. Best of luck. We shall try to keep the Erch away from Arieta. This is as far as they will get."

CHAPTER TWELVE

The Waps fleet began moving soon after. "We are headed for Junica," said Fred. "It is two wormholes away back the way we came. The human fleet was chased away from that system. We expect reinforcements in the next system. We will then attack. We expect the Erch have now been warned by the ships that escaped back through the wormhole. We hope to overcome them by overwhelming force. However we are unlikely to find survivors on Junica."

"Oh. Its that fast, is it?"

"Yes, the Erch are very skilled at overwhelming defenses. There may be survivors on the ground. We may be able to contact them. But our first priority is to destroy their fleets and prevent them spreading," replied Fred.

"But you say that after the Erch take over a planet they begin to build more ships. How do you stop them?"

"We have found the only way to stop them after they have taken over a planet is to destroy that planet," said Fred.

"You mean blow it up!"

"Yes."

"But…but…there might be people left on the ground.….You will destroy all that life!"

"Yes. We have found it was necessary. We found it impossible to wrest the planet back form the Erch if they were entrenched. We might be able to rescue a few survivors. But that is very difficult, and from a military point of view wasteful."

"Oh, no! Oh, Arieta! What can we do?"

"It is possible that as the invasion was in the early stages, and confined to parts of the southern continent, and as the Erch are not receiving reinforcements, the humans can contain them and then destroy them."

John began to feel sick, and he turned away from Fred.

Fred continued, "If it is any consolation, as they say in the films, our devices in other human systems are detecting movements of human fleets. Maybe they will arrive at Arieta soon, with persons you call Space Marines. The people on Arieta display great confidence in them, and joy at their impending arrival. Resistance has been renewed."

"Yes, the Commodore is a very popular person. I hope the joy lasts, and reinforcements arrive soon. Well, lead me back to my cell."

"I regret it is not very comfortable for you. Lacking a shower…"

"Fred, forget the shower! We will cope. It is more not knowing what is going on."

"I considered allowing you on to the bridge, but the captain says that there is no space for you, and you will have to be attached for long periods. He feels that you will be safer in your cabin, and I agree. At least you now have the helmets we obtained form the human ship."

John returned to the cabin to find Norm busy washing clothes in the tiny basin.

"I needed something to do, and the clothes needed cleaning," he said, scrubbing away in the tiny basin.

"We have nowhere to dry them," said John. "I shall ask for a couple of bolts and cords to be put over the loo." He quickly turned and opened the door, and saw Fred disappearing down the corridor.

"Fred!" he yelled.

Fred turned and quickly scuttled back. It was amazing the speed he could do.

"Is there anything wrong?" he asked.

"We need a facility to dry the clothes we have washed," said John.

"Oh. As we do not wear clothing we do not need to wash them. And we were in too much of a hurry to prepare proper facilities."

"It is not your fault. But I suggest a way of drying the clothes. We could put bolts on the walls, and put cords from them and dry the clothes," said John.

"Is that the usual way of drying clothes?"

"On the surface it is. I don't know how it is done on ships. What is the way it is done on human ships, Norm?"

"On the naval ships I have been on, after the clothes are washed, hot air is passed through the clothes until they are dry," he replied.

"Maybe that could be done? Though the air must not be too hot, or it will burn the clothes. Not is excess of 50 degrees centigrade."

Fred soon reappeared with another Waps pushing a wheeled container. Fred explained what was required, the container was filled with damp clothes, and they both disappeared down the corridor.

"So what is happening?" asked Norm.

"I am sorry Norm that you were left down here alone for so long. The Erch fleet has been destroyed."

"I guessed that," said Norm.

"The casualties were twenty per cent of the Waps ships, and one human ship."

"Oh."

"The humans destroyed four Erch ships trying to get though the wormhole, but two escaped."

Norm said nothing, but continued to look sad.

"The human flagship is now in orbit around Arieta. It has landed a troop of one hundred Marines to fight the Erch on the southern continent. The Commander is very popular. The Waps say human reinforcements are on their way. We are now on our way to attack the Erch in the next invaded system, Junica. We will receive reinforcements, but it is expected to be a big battle as they are expecting us. That's about it."

Norm pondered. "Well, we have received our helmets. How many wormholes away is this battle?"

"Two." John noted that Norm seemed to be very pale and wasted. "Have you eaten?" he asked.

"Not much," replied Norm.

"Well I have had nothing, and I am starving. Lets see what food packets we have." John chose some high-energy food with fruit and nuts which Gwen had packed, and persuaded Norm to eat. They sat there having a desultory conversation, chewing their food. "I hate it having nothing to do," said Norm. "At least the washing gave me something to do."

"Well, I'll tell you what I am going to do," said John, "I am going to strip down and have a body bath. The Waps must be dropping a hint when they keep talking about showers." He grabbed a flannel and a towel, stripped down, and washed himself all over, and got dressed. He felt much better after it. He glanced at Norm.

"I have already had one," he said.

They then went through the first wormhole.

"Helmets!" yelled John. They quickly donned the naval style helmets, sat down against the wall, with their feet against the opposite wall.

"This will be fast, if I know the Waps. They don't muck around," said John.

He was right. They quickly went through the second wormhole. This was quickly followed by a sudden thump or clang.

"Debris," said Norm.

The ship began to throw itself around in space, mainly evasive action, with periods of the stasis that they were now used to. There were occasional roars from the weapons. The whole battle seemed to take longer this time, but they eventually settled down to steady movement.

Eventually Fred appeared.

"How did it go, Fred?" asked John.

"Complete victory," said Fred. "Few escaped. If you will accompany me we will go to the bridge and try to contact the planet."

"Can Norm accompany me?" asked John.

"Yes he may, though he must remain careful not to touch anything and stay out of the way of the crew," replied Fred.

The bridge seemed to have received less damage this time. "We need to assess the extent of the Erch occupation of this planet. We have monitored signals. There are two sources of signals we can find so far. Please talk to them."

The first signal was very erratic and difficult to decipher. John discovered that it was again in Spanish. "What can I do?" he thought. "I can do little but give them hope."

John turned to the Captain. "Can I tell them we are a human fleet?"

"Yes, you can. But we cannot rescue them. We have more Erch to attack," the Captain replied.

John replied in Spanish. “Hello, this is the Earth First Fleet. We have destroyed the enemy fleet. More help is coming. What is your situation?”

“Oh, glory to God! Our city is surrounded. We are fighting desperately. Everywhere else is conquered, and is silent. We need help fast. Our city held the army base. The capital city is taken, and we have lost contact. We need help desperately. Can you land reinforcements?”

“I am sorry. We do not have ground troops. The ship which held our Marines was destroyed,” he lied. “Hold out, we have destroyed the enemy fleet, help is coming.”

The second radio communication was in better shape. It came from a small continent on the far side of the world. “All our coastal cities are taken, and we have lost contact with them. We are under attack. These creatures are approaching us from ground and air. They destroy everybody and everything. We do not have much defense. When can we get help?” John gave them the same message he gave the others, but his heart fell. There was nothing he could do for them. There were no other radio communications from the planet.

John turned to the Captain. “Get me out of here.”

On the way back to the cabin, Fred told them that the Waps had lost half their fleet in the battle. Fred explained that these losses were relatively light compared to normal combats of this type. The result was very good. John felt numb, and could only thank

Fred. “Fred, as a representative of the human race, I can tell you that we are deeply grateful for what you are doing for us.”

Norm echoed, “Hear, hear.”

Fred answered, “We are not doing it for you. We are doing it for ourselves. If the Erch became established in this section of the galaxy we would find it difficult to survive.”

“Nevertheless I am deeply grateful. And when all other humans hear and understand what you have done, they will be very grateful too,” replied John.

“Thank you,” replied Fred.

Fred explained that the next system was Norisk, two wormholes away. but they would wait in the system after the first wormhole for reinforcements. After they had destroyed the fleet in the Norilsk system, they would bombard this planet if they saw space ships on the ground, major troop concentrations and where they could assist the survivors.

It was Norm who asked, “Do you think these humans will survive?”

“No,” Fred replied. “Even though we prevent reinforcements, the Erch military force is overwhelming. The humans will be totally destroyed. And eaten. Or what happens, some humans may be kept alive to be eaten later. But the Erch will not make much of an effort to feed or look after their prisoners.”

"What about resistance from individuals?" asked Norm.

"Individual Waps on invaded planets have tried that. But the fundamental problem is food. The Erch eat anything. They are ravenous," replied Fred.

"For a resistance to succeed the fighters have to be fed," Fred continued, as if they had tapped something inside him. "The Erch control access to the planet's surface, so we cannot supply food. We have tried and have never succeeded." Fred waited for a few seconds. "A relation of mine, whom you might call a brother, was landed on an Erch occupied planet to try this sort of resistance. He did not last long. He starved. He could not be rescued."

"Oh, I am so very sorry, Fred," said John.

"Thank you," said Fred, "I am happy the humans are now helping us. Between us we will defeat and destroy the Erchzxxx."

They reached the cabin. Fred said, "If you need anything just open the door."

Inside were their clothes, dry, warm, and neatly folded.

CHAPTER THIRTEEN

"We are on our way again," said John. "We will pick up reinforcements at the next system, and then have another big battle."

Norm looked pale. "Given these sort of percentages I don't rate our chances highly," he said.

"My feeling is that because of us, we are protected. As the original Admiral said, we are placed in a low risk position," replied John.

"Yes, but it is one hell of a battle. The Waps go into it hammer and tongs. They don't hold back," Norm said.

"I am sure we will be all right," said John.

They settled down to wait. "The strain is getting a bit much for Norm," John thought, "and it is beginning to affect his health. He doesn't look too good." He pulled out his reader, and offered Norm a choice of games. They chose an escapist game trying to get to a magic kingdom while fighting dragons and strange creatures. It did not help that Norm's creature kept dying. John offered a game of cards instead.

The ship lurched through the wormhole. "Hmm, obviously a bit of damage there," he thought. The wait in the next system was longer, when they heard obvious repair work being done on the ship. But after a few hours the clangs and drilling ceased.

They accelerated through the next wormhole, and immediately felt stasis. They came out of it, and heard the ship's weapons going full on. Stasis again, more roaring of the weapons, and almost immediate stasis. "What we have stepped into here is a battle a dimension above the previous one," thought John.

At last there was comparative silence. Norm looked spent, just collapsed in a huddle.

"Hey Norm, you must eat something," John said, handing him a candy bar, and a cup of orange juice. He did not respond until John nudged him and said, "Eat!"

He took the bar and automatically began chewing, and sipped the juice.

Eventually the door slid open and Fred stood there. "We have destroyed the Erch, Few escaped," he announced. John felt that his reticulated wasp-like eyes were gleaming. "Do you want to come to the bridge?"

John leapt to his feet, but Norm continued to lie there. "Come on Norm! At least you will get a bit of exercise," John said. Norm struggled to his feet.

John asked, "I hate to ask what our casualties were, Fred."

"If that was a form of a question, we lost half our ships. But their fleet was much bigger. But so was ours."

John made no comment. He was staring at the screen at the planet below.

"Any contacts?"

"None."

"If you want my permission, blow them to smithereens. I know the survivors if any would want it."

"Thank you. We have found suitable targets." After a short delay John saw explosions on the surface of the planet. This continued for about half an hour, flashes continuing all over the globe. "The Waps are obviously doing a through job of it," John thought.

Norm suddenly staggered and sat down on the floor.

"Is Norm ill?" asked Fred.

"Yes, the strain and inactivity is getting to him. He is also not eating. I will help him back to the cabin and make him lie down. And try to get him to eat," John replied.

John staggered back to the cabin, supporting Norm, accompanied by a very concerned Fred.

"I will make him lie down, and try to get him to sleep. Sleep is usually a good cure for this sort of thing." He tucked Norm in to his sleeping bag and told him to close his eyes.

He then sorted through the odds and ends Gwen had packed for him in a hurry, and found among the medicines and some tranquillizers. He filled a cup with some water, lifted Norms head up and forced him to take some tablets. He went out like a light.

"Well, I had better take a rest myself," he thought, turned the light off and climbed into the sleeping bag.

Only to be woken up floating off the floor and held in stasis. As soon as the stasis finished, Norm began shouting and yelling. John zipped out of his sleeping bag, jumped for the light switch and switched the lights on, grabbed the helmets, put one on Norm and the other on himself. Norm's eyes were staring, and dribble was coming out of his mouth. Stasis came on again briefly, and the weapons began to roar.

The battle was briefer this time. Soon things settled down, and eventually Fred reappeared at the door.

"How did things go? Fred," John asked.

"Very successfully, relied Fred. "Their fleet was much smaller this time, and was totally destroyed. We had only one in ten casualties." John could see triumph in Fred's eyes.

"Do you want to come to the bridge?" Fred asked.

"Excuse me, Fred. I had better check Norm." After John had unzipped Norm he saw that Norm had wet his pants, and the inside of the sleeping bag.

"I will take a while to fix up Norm," John said. He took off Norms pants, and piled them in a corner, cleaned him up, and put dry ones on him. He then reversed the sleeping bag, and gave it a wipe, and propped it against the toilet. He then sat Norm down, gave him some food and told him to eat.

"I will be back shortly," he said.

While they were walking along the passage Fred asked, "Is Norm's condition serious?"

"I am not a medical person, but I have heard of people in this condition lapsing into a coma. He needs to be handed over to human care as soon as possible."

By this time they had reached the bridge. The same procedure was conducted as before, and as John watched the destruction on the surface of this nameless planet, John noticed out of the corner of his eye that Fred was conversing with other Waps.

After the destruction had been completed, Fred said to John. "We are concerned with your physical health. Can you continue much longer under these conditions?

"I am feeling fine. I am not affected. I have no physical problems. My concern is for Norm. He is very sick. Maybe because he is much older than me, and maybe because he has had similar battle experiences before. These stresses grow on people. There is a limit that they can take. It looks as if Norm has reached his limit."

"That is unfortunate. But we have a suggestion. This ship is no longer needed in the fleet. We have destroyed the invading fleet as far as we know. We are also getting more reinforcements. Our task is to block the wormholes through which they are coming and hunt down the remnants of the Erch ships. You are needed back in the Arieta system. We have been informed that the human fleet has finally reached Arieta. We need you to return there to talk to them. You shall return in this ship. We will then transfer Norm to one of their ships."

"Excellent," said John. "I hope that the fleet is placing troops on the surface of the planet to fight the Erch. However I have one suggestion."

"When this ship returns it must be accompanied by a Waps fleet as least as large as the human fleet. I hope you can spare them. They may be damaged and ships in bad fighting condition. The humans will not know that."

"Why do you ask this?" asked Fred.

"You must immediately impress the humans. Gain their respect. This is important as this is the beginning of a major diplomatic initiative. It must start well. That is how humans think. If humans do not respect you they will not listen to you. They need a little bit of fear. Now I am beginning to understand Waps. You will say, what is the point? The humans must understand that the Waps have a big fleet out there. But unless they see one, that thought will not register."

"I understand," said Fred. "It is the same as when you insisted on device which visibly picked balls to choose the arbitrators instead of having a simple random number generator."

"Exactly!"

There was extensive humming among the Waps, and communications with the flagship or fleet commanders.

Eventually Fred said, "We can spare ships to the number of known human ships in the Arieta system. They will accompany you. You will return and negotiate."

"One, last thing, do I have a free hand? It is possible that these negotiations might have to be conducted on Earth, accompanied by your fleet again," John asked.

There was further humming among the Waps.

"We have great faith in you. You will be accompanied by myself, of course. Others will be transferred to this ship, who have authority. The deal is that you will negotiate until you are stopped. If you feel that you may ask us anything, do so freely. Is that understood?"

"Understood."

Arieta floated below them again. "How are things going down there?" asked John.

"The human fleet is landing what you call Space Marines near Sevilla. The humans have lost much of the western part of the continent, and the city of Sevilla is under attack. After some initial setbacks the Space Marines are beginning to hold their own. They need more reinforcements and these have been requested. Other fleets are coming, but their approach is slow. I do not consider that the humans have really understood their danger."

"They will eventually. From my knowledge of human wars, they will take six months to get into gear, and nine months before really fighting back. You say the wormholes are blocked, and no more can arrive?"

"Hopefully."

"Well, it is a going to be a bloody surface war. The humans will grind on until they succeed, or are totally defeated. Lets talk to the fleet."

There was already a voice communicating with them. The human fleet was already in battle position.

"Hello, this is John Griffin of the Waps fleet. Is Commodore Jackson there?"

There was confusion at the other end.

"Who is that?" asked a voice.

"Hello, this is John Griffin of the Waps fleet, is Commodore Jackson there?'

"Waps?"

"Yes, Waps, your allies remember?"

There was further discussion. "Hello, this is Vice Admiral Smith here."

"Any chance of speaking to the Admiral in charge?"

"Well – he is busy at the moment."

"Fine. Well, the first thing I want to settle is – see that debris out there. Of two massive fleets. The Waps claim them as salvage. All of it."

"What, why? This is a human system."

"Yes, but half that stuff is the remains of Waps ships. The other half is the remains of Erch ships. Now the Waps wish to analyze the Erch ships for technological advance. You would not be able to understand them."

"We don't see why we should allow you…"

"Any attempt to salvage this debris without Waps permission will be fired on."

There was silence.

"We don't like that."

"We are sorry. But under the circumstances…."

A new voice interrupted. "This is Admiral Malcolm."

"Hello, Admiral."

"What is your fleet doing back here?"

"We have returned to see how well you are coping with the Erch. Also to make arrangements to accompany your ships to the other captured planets."

"Accompany?"

"No fighting is involved, at least in space. We have destroyed the Erch in human space."

"All of them?"

"As many as we can find. You may have to fight the odd one."

"Oh. The Waps have done this for us?"

"No. For themselves. However if you want to recapture the captured planets, you will have to do that for yourselves. My main concern now is the forge an agreement so that Waps and human ships can operate together if necessary."

"An agreement?"

"Yes. It may not have escaped you that very large Waps fleets are knocking around in human space. This one is one of many, much bigger than any human fleet. It is necessary to come to an agreement so that any incident does not devolve into fighting."

"Oh. Many Waps fleets?"

"Yes. But the Waps wish to be friendly. Remember they have destroyed the Erch fleets for you."

"In all the systems?"

"As far as we know."

"I will have to communicate with Earth."

"Of course. In the mean time, we will move our fleet further out to prevent incidents. Let me know when you have received a reply. However there is one personal request."

"What is that."

"We have another human adviser on board. His name is Commander Norman Foster. He has met Commodore Jackson in person. Anyway he is now in a near coma, and seriously ill. We wish to transfer him to a human vessel for medical treatment. Is that possible?"

"I don't see why not," was the reply. "How do you propose to do it?"

"We do not have human space suits. However we have a skiff ten meters long and four meters wide. We can place Commander Foster in it, and the skiff can enter an airlock."

"Hmmm. I will designate a ship to take him. When can it be done?"

"Thirty minutes. A ship needs to maneuver near to our ship and open a brightly lit port."

"It will be done."

Norm was carried on a stretcher to the port and placed in the skiff. Before he left, John said to him, "Norm, you are being taken to a human ship. If you get back to the Line, can you do something for me? Go and see my wife Gwen and tell her the last time you saw me, I was fine and in good health."

Norm cracked a smile and said, "Sure. Best of luck."

After Norm had left, John turned to Fred. "Norm deserves an extra thousand kilos of gold. Transfer a thousand kilos of gold from my account if you have it."

Fred replied, "That will not be necessary. We have already credited him with more than two thousand kilos of gold."

CHAPTER FOURTEEN

"What happens now?" asked Fred.

"We sit and wait," replied John. "We need to find an orbit, say at about the orbit of the next planet out, so the humans do not feel threatened. Then we wait. The military are different from traders. They are not motivated to get a fast result. They will discuss and decide among themselves. They will also send to Earth for advice. They are mainly motivated to do nothing wrong. I am sure all the ships in the Waps fleet have repairs to do, and perhaps these can be carried out while we are waiting. You have to be patient."

"Oh, and another thing," continued John, "you will have to remain well away from the incoming wormhole. The human reinforcements will not be expecting you. I suggest that you put a broadcasting unit near the wormhole broadcasting a message. I could record it for you if you like."

He did that, explaining that the Waps were allies and no threat. This was set to repeat.

New human ships came in, and others departed, while the Waps waited and conducted their repairs. There was no attempt to contact them. John could guess about the frantic activity in the human fleet, and the quandary the human Admiral was in.

Also the pressure poor Norman was under. They would certainly be grilling him on everything he knew. He would probably be on one of the departing ships.

Eventually another major human fleet turned up, and a message was received that the humans would like a discussion.

“Insist that the discussions be conducted on a Waps vessel, the largest you have,” said John. “Talk to them yourself. They will try to bully me.”

There was a lot of talking back and forth, until the humans agreed. “They are asking how many people can they bring?” said Fred.

“As many as practicable,” replied John. “What is the largest size vessel which can enter the pressurized hold of the flagship?”

There was further discussion in terms of meters, and the human response was somewhat subdued when they learnt that the flagship could swallow an Earth destroyer. The humans agreed to send a dozen human negotiators.

“It will probably end up a bit more. You will need to impress them. Do you have a large vehicle to collect them to contain fifteen persons, suitably modified. Send the vehicle at high speed on a large circuitous route, ending in a large room. They will then face fifteen Waps, even though you may not need so many. And do you need me?”

“Of course we need you. Your advice as always is invaluable”, answered Fred, waving an arm animatedly.

"Well tell me when the meeting is. I shall go back to my cabin to wash and change. I need a shave. I will also need to be taken to this meeting room early," he said finally.

John could not discern what the original purpose of the room was, but it was large and impressive. Fifteen cloth-covered benches with backs were set up opposite them, and a similar type of bench was set up on the Waps side.

"May I make a suggestion?" asked John.

"Of course."

"The humans will be happier and at ease if they sat at a table. A long one. When they sit it must reach stomach height. I will sit and show you." He did, and demonstrated the height. "You can either lower one of your tables, or rest the chairs on a slight platform."

"Which do you prefer?"

"That you lower the height of the table."

The Waps hummed as the discussed, and soon a number of tables were brought in and placed end to end. "They will now have to be reduced in height by exactly the same height. I shall demonstrate." He drew up the chair and sat in front of a table, demonstrating the distance to be lowered. The Waps then set to and lowered the tables exactly as required.

"Is anything else needed?" asked Fred.

"A cloth covering for the table is sometimes used, together with carafes and cups of water, but these are not necessary. They are unlikely to drink the water."

There was further humming and even these appeared, quickly and efficiently.

While the Waps waited, John first asked which of the Waps will be talking, and their titles. "Titles are important to humans. They need a hierarchy."

Fred said, "Call me chief adviser." He pointed to others. "This is the Admiral. Chief representative of the home government. Chief strategist. Vice Admiral. We decide very much as a group."

"Try to make these titles impressive as possible. I will ask you to introduce yourselves."

He then explained the situation to them. "The humans first of all strongly require information. The attack by the Erch was a total surprise for them. The presence of the Waps is a total surprise for them. Their main motive is to send the fleet through the wormholes and check the other planets. They still suspect that they were attacked by the Waps, and you are allies of the Erch. There are a lot of enemies of the Waps back on Earth. Attitudes will not change until it is clearly demonstrated that it was the Erch and not the Waps who were the ones who attacked them."

"What shall we do?" asked Fred.

"It depends on what you want from the humans," replied John. "If you want nothing you can announce that you have destroyed the Erch on this side of the rift. When you feel that the humans can control the wormholes to prevent the Erch entering human space, you will go home."

"What will be the consequences of that?" asked Fred.

"When the humans realize that the Waps have saved Arieta, and prevented the Erch entering human space, they will become more friendly. Don't expect gratitude, but they will be less antagonistic. Maybe they will allow Waps to travel in human space on human ships."

"What if we want more?" replied Fred.

"Like what?" asked John.

"With human assistance we may be able to conquer and destroy the Erch," said Fred.

"Then you must get the humans very, very angry; very angry indeed, with the Erch."

"Back to your anger. It is a powerful motive for humans."

"Yes it is," replied John.

"How do you do that?" asked Fred.

"The humans must be invited to accompany you to the conquered human planets. I know you will think this illogical, but the humans must be invited by you to jointly land on these planets in an attempt to wrest the planets back from the Erch. Maybe they will find survivors, maybe not. But what they will see, what the Erch have done to the humans, will make them very, very angry. Very angry indeed. White hot furious. It will be slow to grow, but in one year's time the entire human kind will be prepared to devote all its resources to eradicate the Erch. You will have a devoted friend and ally."

The Waps were silent for a while. Then they began to hum among themselves.

Fred said, "As you have previously said, it is the way it is said to them."

"It is much more Fred, they have to see with their own eyes."

The human delegation entered the room soon afterwards. It seemed to be a group of military and civilians. Some of them gave John dirty looks.

John rose. "Please make yourselves comfortable. The water is completely potable. I can demonstrate if necessary"

"That won't be necessary. And you are?" the military person in the center chair asked.

"My name is John Griffin. I am adviser to the Waps. Some of the Waps have translators. I suggest that those with translators introduce themselves." Which they did, interspersing Waps military titles with titles Lord and High.

"My name is Admiral Malcolm, this is Admiral Wrexham of the Third Fleet, Secretary Brunnley of the Department of Foreign Affairs, Robert Sim of the Xenology Bureau, ..." And he continued down the table.

"Thank you for coming to this meeting," John replied, "I am the usual spokesman for the Waps. You may call the Waps on my right Fred, though he is very senior in the Waps hierarchy. Fred may intervene or explain from time to time. The others may intervene or may state a point, but they generally communicate with Fred, who communicates with me. Is that process clear? Something like the Lowells of Boston…Oh, never mind! Now why do you want to see us?"

"We are concerned with your fleet. Why is it sitting here?"

"The fleet is recuperating. The Waps fleet, which this is just a part, has had several battles with the Erch in the systems up ahead. We have also been sent back here to escort your fleet through to these systems to make sure there are no mishaps, and you do not accidentally fall into conflict with the Waps fleet," John replied.

"Escort?" asked the senior Admiral.

"Yes, if that is all you want, yes. A few of our ships could accompany your fleet to the systems of Junica and Norisk, and you can view for yourselves the damage the Erch have done to these planets."

"Damage?"

"That is an understatement. The Erch have completely destroyed the populations of the planets Junica and Norisk and beyond. Destroyed completely. They are all dead. Eaten too," John said.

"Eaten? I don't believe that!" Secretary Brunley exclaimed.

"You are well aware of what is happening on the southern continent of Arieta. Not only have the Erch killed everybody on one half the continent, they have eaten them as well. Or don't you believe your hard-pressed Marines?" John hazarded, but he had a pretty good guess of the events now occurring on the surface.

There was an uncomfortable silence. "We are investigating these claims," said Secretary Brunley.

"Personally I hope?" asked John sarcastically.

The man blushed.

The Admiral grimaced. "The Waps claim to be enemies of the Erch?"

"Yes. As the wide area of debris in this system attest. They destroyed a fleet larger than the combined size of your fleets. As the records of the Arieta government attest."

"It was quite a battle," one of the officers down the table said.

"It was one hell of a battle," replied John, "as were three others in the other systems. As well as the one where we saved Commodore Jackson's fleet. Four in all."

The navy people glanced at each other.

"Are the Erch fleets totally destroyed?"

"As far as we know. However sooner or later the human fleets must take over guarding the entry wormholes. But in the short-term do you want to be escorted to view the planets Junica and Norisk? We can do that for you. Also with the agreement of Fred and his colleagues, we may be able to assist in landings on these planets for you to check on the status of the inhabitants."

Fred said, "We will assist with human landings on these planets."

"Finally," asked the Admiral, "does the Waps fleet threaten us?"

"We will stay well away from you. We await your command. If you can spare troops or a landing party, we will escort you to these planets and prevent the Erch attacking you."

"Is this correct?" said the Admiral, looking at Fred.

"We entirely concur," said Fred. "We will assist you with landing on those planets to the best of our ability." There was humming from the other Waps. Three of them said, "We agree."

"Thank you," said the Admiral, somewhat relieved. "We will let you know our decision."

"And you are welcome to visit our ship at any time," said John.

"And you ours," replied the Admiral.

"I believe I am still a fugitive," said John, looking at the civilian.

CHAPTER FIFTEEN

The combined fleets orbited the planet Junica. New Marine reinforcements had arrived on other fleets, and despite desperate pleas by the defenders of Sevilla, a detachment had been sent with the fleet to attempt exploratory landing on Junica and Norisk..

The landing party included members of the media. John had maneuvered a contingent of media onto the fleet. His machinations started as soon as he had returned from the meeting on the flagship over a month before. He had said to Fred, "Try a get me to speak to the President of Arieta."

John did most of the talking. He talked to various officials in Spanish by radio, saying who he was and he was talking from the Waps fleet. Finally he got through to the President.

"Hello, Senor Presidente, this is José Fernandez, the human adviser with the Waps fleet."

"Buenos Dias, Senor Fernandez," replied the President guardedly.

"The purpose of our conversation is that I would like to inform you that the Waps have invited the human fleet to inspect the situation at Junica and other planets which have been invaded by Waps." John knew perfectly well that the call was being monitored by the media.

"Also I have a personal interest in the city of Sevilla. I resided there until recently, with the name also of Peter Brown. How are things going there? Can you tell me please?"

"Not good," replied the President. "The city is under siege. We desperately need reinforcements."

"I have some advice for you. My impression is that the humans in command still do not believe that the Erch are eating humans. If you facilitate the travel to Sevilla of the many media people who are now in your capital, the truth will be known. Earth will send many more Space Marines."

"But Senor, I have been told not to send the media! They can't defend them!" replied the President frantically.

John raised his voice, and waved his hands. "Send them anyway. The Erch must have eaten at least two million of your citizens so far. You must go yourself! And take all the media who want to go with you! It is a matter of honor! You do not want to be thought a coward!" John yelled.

The President jumped, and waved his hands. "Senor, I am not a coward! I am the President! Yes, I will go! Yes, immediately!"

"Bueno! You will save the citizens of Sevilla!"

The President went, with local reinforcements, and the media. The results they found were heartbreaking. In previously Erch occupied areas, no survivors. Just gnawed bones of men, women and children. The media were taken to one of

Sevilla's recaptured abattoirs, and presented with the sight of hundreds of human corpses, de-gutted, hanging from hooks, while many were dismembered, processed, and placed in storage containers. They were shown one production line where babies were processed and their dismembered bodies were placed in small containers. Obviously a culinary specialty. Many of the media crew could not take this, and ran out. The President was escorted around, and went as white as a sheet. He was shaking as he left.

The media reports went by communications carriers to Earth, and massive reinforcements soon poured in. The situation in Sevilla was stabilized, and they began to push back. Demands from the media to accompany the fleet was overwhelming, and despite warnings of danger, media representatives were scattered among the fleet.

John farewelled the President, who was literally crying on the phone, and wishing John "God speed". There were many relatives on Junica, another Spanish speaking planet. He finished, "Oh your gold, senor, I have prevented its removal from the planet."

"Thank you, Senor Presidenté. As soon as you are able, please return it all to the bank it was taken from. That will help restore confidence in the community," replied John.

The landing was at Junica's capital Barca. The landing fleet was attacked with intense fire and flying craft. It was only with the assistance of the firepower of the fleet that they managed to land. Some intrepid media types volunteered to go with them.

John observed from the Waps ship. “I am not an expert in this, but I don’t think the Marines have much of a chance of staying down there for long, much less getting back safely.”

That seemed to be the opinion of the Earth fleet, by the way their intervention intensified. Members of the fleet went down low to provide covering fire in a wide perimeter around the landing party, which was apparently fighting intensely with Erch attacking them on the ground.

After a few hours the attacking party retreated back to their vessels and took off, heading back to their ships. By this time attacks had even intensified, regardless of the covering fire provided by the hovering ships.

“Not good,” thought John. “I hate to think of the casualties.”

“I wonder what their results were,” John asked himself. He turned to Fred. “Fred, give them twelve hours and then ask the humans if they found any civilian survivors. This should prompt them with some summary of their result.”

Even before the twelve hours were up, communication missiles were heading back through the wormhole to Sevilla. “They must have found something,” John thought.

John was in his cabin when Fred appeared. “John, the human stay on the ground, though brief, allowed them to do some exploration. They found in the surrounding buildings blood and dried human bones with Erch tooth marks. They found no human survivors alive," he said.

"Do the humans intend to return to the surface?" John asked.

"There is some debate on this, but the human casualties were substantial," Fred replied.

It transpired that it was decided that as there was another planet to visit, they could not risk more casualties, and decided not to make a further landing. The planet proceed to the next planet Norisk.

The same scenario played itself out, though this time fewer media people volunteered to accompany the Marines. If anything the intensity of the firepower was worse, and the stay briefer. There was the same result. Gnawed human bones, and no sign of survivors.

This time the human fleet meted retribution of the planet below, and rained fire on any Erch concentration they could find. The mood of the fleet had entirely changed.

Around the third planet, the combined fleets orbited. There was a debate going among the humans whether there should be a third landing on another planet, and if so, what size and where it should be.

John was sitting in the bridge watching the planet below. Suddenly there was a flurry of alarm among the Waps, and high-pitched alarms began to sound.

John was seized by Fred. Four strong pinions grabbed him, carried him to a chair and strapped him in. “Erch attack,” were Fred’s brief words.

“Let me warn the Earth fleet!” screamed John.

Fred darted back to the controls, grabbed a small microphone, flicked a couple of switches in a blink of an eye, gave the microphone to John, and said “Speak.”

John just screamed into the microphone, “Emergency! Emergency! Erch attack. Action Stations! Attention. Erch fleet attacking” Emergency!...” He kept screaming into the phone without waiting for a response, until he felt the usual stasis. The Waps were by now strapped in. Lights were flashing on consoles. He could feel the roaring sound as the weapons resounded. At one point there was a crack, not a bang like the previous occasion, the ship leapt aside, and stasis occurred. The roaring intensified and the lights flickered.

John just clutched the side of his seat, his mouth open, his mouth drooling. After a while a thought came, “This seems to be going on longer than before.” But eventually the sound died down, thing returned to what John felt was near normal. There was a lot of humming among the Waps, and numerous communications. John just tried to relax. “It’s all over. It’s all over. Relax, relax, relax…” he told himself while staring into the distance.

Eventually he felt someone standing beside him. It was Fred. “How are you, John?”

"I'm fine," replied John. He then noticed that one of Fred's arms seemed to be damaged. "What's happened to you, Fred?"

"I am fine," replied Fred. "This damage can be easily repaired."

"Have we won the battle?" John asked.

"Yes," said Fred, "thanks to the human fleet. They attacked what you can call the flank of the Erch fleet. Without concern for casualties. To use human terms, they tore into them. I don't think the Erch has ever experienced such an attack. They turned to face the humans, which gave us the opportunity to attack them and defeat them. A few surviving Erch were driven off."

"Yes, Fred. The humans were furious after what they saw on those planets. Now you know the effect of human anger," said John.

"I can see that now. We will remember it. We are also very grateful. If it wasn't for the human intervention the Erch would certainly have destroyed us. As it is our casualties are very heavy. And over half the human fleet has been destroyed."

"I am very sorry to hear that Fred." John pondered. "Now you must go through a process which humans expect."

"What is that?" asked Fred.

"You must express gratitude to the humans," answered John.

"We do express gratitude for service. The humans have gained major credit with us."

John laughed.

"No, your Admiral must go to the human Admiral in his ship. He must personally state that he is very grateful to the humans for saving their fleet. Furthermore, the Waps Admiral must extend one hand and ask if he can shake the Admiral's hand. This has vast symbolic importance to the humans. From now on the two species are close friends. Finally while the Admirals are shaking hands the Waps Admiral must say these words, "Now we are allies." Do you get all that, Fred?"

"Recorded and transmitted. It will be done," said Fred. "But what will be the consequences?"

"Humans will just love the Waps. They will be able to move freely on human worlds. People will come up to them all the time to shake their hands. The Waps will have to be prepared for that. But more importantly humans will be prepared to operate joint fleets with the Waps against the Erch, even in Erch space. They will have only one aim, eradicate the Erch. And Fred, with Waps help, they will do it."

Fred just hummed, but stood there saying nothing.

CHAPTER SIXTEEN

The return trip started uneventfully. It was decided not to pursue the Erch through more wormholes. Both fleets had been severely mauled, and after a careful search for survivors the fleet turned for home. This time the fleet was mixed together, with the damaged vessels, both Human and Waps, in the center of the fleet, and the strongest vessels at the rear. John was not concerned over the position of his vessel. All he wanted was some sleep.

The news of the battle had been sent ahead of course, as had the news of the previous landings on Junica and Norisk. John could imagine their reception as the news reached Arieta, then Earth, and then quickly spread out among all inhabited planets. First disbelief and antagonism, calls for corroboration, to be replaced by shock, anger and fury. John knew that by the time the combined fleet reached Arieta, reinforcements would be pouring in, and all human space would be on an intense war footing. If the Waps had underestimated the humans, they would be in for a surprise.

When the combined fleet reached the system of Junica, they met a human fleet coming the other way. The human Admiral of their fleet announced that he was going to consult the Admiral of the other fleet.

Fred observed, "It is inadvisable for them to take the route we have taken. An Erch fleet is pursuing us. Given the likely comparative strengths, the human fleet will be destroyed."

"How do you know, Fred?" asked John.

"We left devices behind. They detected the Erch fleet and shot ahead to warn our fleet," Fred replied.

"What do you suggest?" asked John.

"We have requested reinforcements. They are coming through other wormholes, and will shortly arrive here. As this system is a strategic location, I suggest that we wait here. Take a stand as you say. Hopefully the reinforcements will arrive before the Erch fleet. "

"And if we do get wiped?"

"Then Arieta is in serious danger. Depending on the size of the Erch fleet, it may be lost."

"Give me the phone. Let me talk to the Admiral. This is going to be our Waterloo."

"And the Waps the Prussians. Lets hope General Blucher arrives in time," replied Fred. His humming seemed to be laughter.

John thought, "I am absolutely sure the bugger has a sense of humor."

"Admiral Adelfo speaking," said the voice on the phone.

"Hello, this is John Griffin, the Waps' liaison person. They inform me that we are being pursued by a large Erch fleet, and if your other human fleet goes back the way we came, they will be totally destroyed."

There was silence. "You are absolutely sure of this?"

"They have detection devices, and I always believe the Waps. I have always found them totally truthful, and never exaggerate."

"Furthermore," continued John, "they tell me that they will be getting reinforcements to this system shortly. Fred, can you tell me the size of these reinforcements please?" he said, turning to Fred.

"It is one of our larger fleets. It has fifteen of our largest ships, forty two battle cruisers, seventy or more destroyers of the type we are in now, flankers and interceptors, what you call frigates, over two hundred of them, and many small missile firing and scouting vessels."

"When will it arrive?"

"Two days hence. Through the wormhole both sides have designated D4. The Erch are coming through D3, at an unspecified time, but are not earlier than a day after us."

"What do you suggest we do?" asked the Admiral.

Fred replied. "We must wait here. We must defend wormhole D1, otherwise the will reach Arieta. Depending on the size of the Erch fleet, Arieta could be lost permanently. If we take up station near wormhole D1, we will have tactical and defensive superiority. We may be able to hold them off until the reinforcements arrive."

More silence. "I will discuss this with the other Admiral. But I need to tell you that I am originally from Arieta."

The combined fleets took up station at wormhole D1 and waited. The fleets were not mixed, but kept at separate locations. The human fleet blocked the wormhole, with Admiral Adelfo's fleet at the center of the wormhole. Nothing was going to get through, he announced, and he sounded if he meant it. Weak and damaged ships had been sent through the wormhole, with the badly injured, with desperate requests for reinforcement. Indeed they were beginning to arrive, in a steady trickle. In a circle round Admiral Adelfo's fleet was the second human fleet, and in a circle around them was third circle of the Waps fleet, extending forward and forming a concave shell. Fire could be sprayed inward. It was a very good defensive position. The Erch would have to attack to get through, or turn around and go home.

The wait was grim. John was kept on hand to answer queries from the fleet, but the human fleet command obviously knew what to do. They had beacons near wormhole D3. At the first flicker they would be alerted.

And the first flicker did occur, a day and a half later. Scout boats flicked in and out, and then the

Erch fleet poured through, and began orbiting the sun, far out in its Oort cloud. It obviously intended to head directly for wormhole D1, and ignore the planet Junica.

"Damn!" John thought. "Another twelve hours, or if they delayed at Junica, we would have got them."

"Fred, what is the size of the Erch fleet?" asked John.

"About ten per cent larger than ours, but the ships are better than the human fleet," replied Fred. "However we are in a very powerful defensive position."

"What are our chances?"

"Very little if the Waps fleet does not arrive in time. However if they do, the Erch will be caught between us and almost totally destroyed."

"Do you have any last instruction for the human fleet?"

"Only tell them to hold their positions unless ordered otherwise. And all humanity expects ever person to do their duty," replied Fred.

John looked at Fred. "Poetry!" he thought. "Where does Fred get it from?"

He contacted the Admiral. He said, "Here are the instructions from the Waps High Command. Hold your positions unless ordered otherwise. And all humanity expects every person to do their duty."

The instructions rippled through the human fleet. There was a roll of replies "We will!".

The Erch put their heaviest ships at the front, expecting to punch their way through the fleet. It entered a cone of fire, concentrated at its peak. Only the Erch at their fleet's outer surface could fire back, which reduced their firepower, while the allied fleet structure was designed so that all could supply un-interrupted fire.

Despite their size, the Erch frontal battalions dissolved, to be replaced by second and third lines. These dissolved also. John was watching all this on a screen set up for him in the control room. Eventually the Erch fleet slowed, and backed away from the combined fire of the cone. It waited, then like a flower unfurling, sections peeled off the attack the wall of the allied fleet. The human fleet was ready for this, and began to form mini-cones around the salients of the attacking fleets. Where the attack seemed to be succeeding, the Waps fleet detached ships of its own and sent them to help. Eventually these tongues of attack withdrew, to reform and attack elsewhere on the wall. The allied casualties were obviously mounting, and John wandered how long they could take this.

Eventually John felt his own ship move to fly into the flaming maelstrom. The armaments rumbled, there was intermittent stasis, and bangs which were obviously near misses. "How long can we keep this up?" he thought.

The heat inside the Waps ship massively increased. It felt as if he was baking in an oven. Over 150 degrees. This did not seem to affect the Waps, but the heat left John sweating and gasping. He felt a cold wet cloth being placed over him, which in turn warmed and dried. But keeping it wrapped around him, and avoiding metal parts, he could survive while watching the battle on the screen.

Then John noticed a change in the structure of the Erch fleet. It seemed as if it was a swarm of bees that had collectively decided to fly the other way. If anything the activity of his own ship intensified. Then the screen was suddenly switched to a more distant view, and he saw another fleet sweeping down on them.

"Is this Blucher?" croaked John.

He heard Fred's voice rumble "Yes. And just in time too."

By this time, the Erch fleet was heading for the other wormholes. Any undefended ones. They had lost any semblance of group tactics. The Waps descended upon them with a fury that was a wonder to behold. They took control of all the wormholes aside from D1, and Erch had to fight to get though them. The Waps formed a tunnel through which the Erch had to fly, being fired on without relent. Other Erch were being chased around the system until many fled out into interstellar space. They had a long trip to the next system if they made it.

The temperature began to rapidly fall. Fred appeared. "I'm sorry about the heat. We should have realized that the intense heat caused by the battle would reduce our ability to remove heat from the ship in that direction. The ship quickly heated up. I hope this situation this did not unduly affect the human fleet."

The human fleet, it transpired, was relatively unaffected. Human ships had been designed to radiate sudden bursts of heat, or absorb it, and the humans were only discomforted at the most. Those that survived.

"Well, survived again," thought John, "I am really beating the odds. But I am not cut out for life in the navy. When do I get home?"

The meeting of the Admirals, Waps and human, was more of a group hug than a discussion of the outcomes. The casualties were terrible. One third of the human fleet was gone. A quarter of the Waps'. But the humans did not seem to care. A guard of Waps and a few human ships was placed over the wormhole, and the exultant though shattered fleet descended upon Arieta. Soon the news spread throughout human and Waps space. The quote "All humanity expects every person to do their duty" was attributed to John, though he tried to explain it was really Fred. Nobody believed him.

Back at the Arieta system, John could feel the joy several thousand kilometers out in space. The ether crackled with delirious congratulatory messages aimed at the fleet. John watched some of the broadcasts. The entire population seemed to be hysterical, running around cheering without stop.

By this time the Waps and human ships were mixed up together, and there seemed no attempt to separate them. John was dragged to a council of war in the human Admiral's ship, together with Fred.

It was a boardroom table, along which the humans and the Waps attempted to sit side by side. An attempt had been made to construct Waps' seats, and make them comfortable.

Admiral Adelfo began by heaping praise on the Waps for helping to save Arieta. He obviously had a personal interest in this. The Waps replied in their measured way that they were doing it to protect themselves. If the Erch established themselves in this part of the galaxy they were doomed.

The humans took this as modesty and heaped more praise on the Waps.

The Admiral read out the congratulations from the Earth Government. It had been completely converted to the enormity of the threat, and the relief was transparent.

The Admiral than coughed and asked "What are we going to do now?"

John had been briefed by Fred on this, and had discussed the situation with the Waps High Command.

John perked up. "On behalf of the Waps, and as you may have noticed they are unable to express themselves well in Earth terms, they regard themselves to be in a committed and unbreakable alliance with the humans against the Erch. In particular, in this war area, they will supply a segment of their fleet to guard Arieta, and prevent the return of the Erch. They will fully cooperate with the human fleet to do this. In a short while I can discuss a formal mechanism where this cooperation will be formalized. Any disputes will go to a form of arbitration." John smiled at this and thought about the arrangements made on The Line. "In the medium to long term, as soon as the human fleet has recovered its strength, the Waps invite joint patrols in strength to seek out the Erch on this side of the rift, destroy them, and drive them back to the other side of the wormholes which they use to enter this side of the rift. Eventually to block these wormholes from further entry. I know I have said a lot. I first turn to Fred, who despite his name, is a very highly placed member of the WAPS government, look on him as equivalent to Deputy Admiral, to confirm what I said."

Fred replied "I confirm what John said, except for one detail. John has wrongly promoted me. I am a member of the civilian government."

There was laughter around the table. The atmosphere was much more relaxed now.

The first question was "What about the human planets, Junica, and Norisk and others…?"

Fred and John looked at each other.

Fred answered. "Our experience with captured planets is that despite a great deal of effort we were unable to recapture them. In the end we had to destroy them, to prevent them being used by the Erch. We will assist you with our naval craft if you attempt to recapture these planets, but we do not regard your chances of success very highly. In the case of Arieta, you have a much better chance of success. But you will find them dug in, and difficult to remove without much loss of life. Their characteristics are very much like one of the insects you have on Earth, the ant. But very intelligent, totally logical, and incapable of recognizing any different type of intelligent life has the right to live."

There was silence after Fred had imparted this information.

There were further questions and discussions. Then John announced, "Before this meeting breaks up, I would like to suggest a formal method of liaison between the two fleets. Instead of this radio contact between Admirals, which with the best will in the world, tends to break down, I would like to suggest that all communications, requests, and initial planning should go through a group which I would like to give the title "The Joint Committee." This will be very high level, and even your government on Earth must go through this committee in all its communications with the Waps. Sub committees, such as military and tactical committees should be appointed subordinate to the Joint Committee."

John caught his breath and looked around. There was no response. "The initial Joint Committee, and this is what the Waps want, is a three person committee to discuss all matters, including fleet issues. The initial location will be a small vessel provided by the government of Arieta, connected on each side by a human and a Waps vessel, to accommodate members of each specie's committee. In orbit around Arieta."

John took another breath and looked around.

"Eventually this Joint Committee will be transferred to Earth, to be replaced by a military sub committee."

Admiral Adolfo replied "This sounds good. I shall discuss it with Earth."

John replied, "Thank you. I have not quite finished yet. With the best will in the world, disagreements occur and cannot be resolved by the committee. After the Joint Committee has been set up, the Waps also want a system of arbitration set up, along the lines of what now operates at the Line. The Waps have used it for a number of years, and are pleased with the way it operates. Since the Waps and human mindsets are totally different, normal human diplomatic processes will not work. The Waps will like to set up this process to resolve disputes, including the random ball selection machine, no matter how strange it appears to humans."

The Admiral replied, "I will transmit this request to Earth." The meeting broke up very cordially.

John also received a batch of letters from Gwen. She had sent letters via the Waps, and a number had accumulated.

Gwen's communications were disconsolate. She was very worried about stories of battles, and the updates from the Waps, together with reassurances that he had survived, did not make her happy. She was in a perpetual state of anguish, and this came through, though she tried to be chatty about the children. In later letters she began talking about travelling to Arieta, or at least Earth, to be near him. John decided against that, as he thought it was dangerous. Some dangerous person would try to use Gwen against him. Also the war situation looked bad. If the Erch broke through, the Line would be the only safe place left, as it was protected by the Waps.

He replied "Darling Gwen, I love you like crazy and miss you sorely. Tell Hugh and Emma that Dad loves them, and be good to Mum. He will soon be back. You may have heard of big battles. I am unscathed. The Erch were defeated. However Fred tells me that there are big Erch fleets out there in human space, and things are still very dangerous. Arieta is on the front line, and partly occupied by Erch. If it was just you, I would say come, and we would be on the ship together as usual. But you have to keep the children safe. The safest place is the Line. The Waps will look after you and keep you safe. Even from that horrible Rick if he manages to get out of prison. Stay safe my darling. Give my kisses to the children. Love and many kisses, John."

He wandered if he would ever see them again.

CHAPTER SEVENTEEN

"Fred, is there any chance of my setting foot on Arieta?" John asked.

"You wish to land on Arieta?" Fred replied.

"Yes. I really do need a break. Get out in the sunshine. Eat some decent food. Even have a shower. Maybe I can even visit Sevilla."

"Is this necessary for your health?"

"Yes. If I stay in this ship much longer, I shall end up like Norman."

"We shall be sorry to lose you."

"I promise to return. I promise. But I desperately need a break."

"I shall see what can be done."

And as good as his word, he arranged for John to land on Arieta. After further discussions it was decided that in order to prevent the human fleet holding on to him, John would be sent as an envoy to the Arieta government. The President was contacted and asked if he would like José Fernandez to visit him. He fell over himself to extend an invitation.

In due course, a Waps shuttle landed John at the Merida spaceport. There was a large welcome delegation, and John felt rather scruffy, as well as smelling of liquid from his cabin's sanitary toilet. Nobody seemed to notice it, and all were desperate the shake his hand. He was met by the President in person, then the head of their military, and then representatives of the Earth fleet. He was then whisked in an open topped limousine in a cavalcade through the avenues, past lines of crowds, to an expensive hotel. He was told there would be a grand dinner in his honor that night.

"I would love a dinner, but I have nothing suitable to wear!" said John.

"All will arranged," he was told, and sure enough tailors came to measure him up for clothing.

John said, "I will pay, but I need a whole list of things from underclothes to a new set of everyday clothes."

"Oh no, Senor! Anything for you. At government expense."

That evening he was attired in formal clothes, white tie and tails, and taken to a banqueting hall. He certainly enjoyed the magnificent food, which he tore into. He explained that the food on the ship was very limited and plain. There were questions about his life on the Waps ship, and the battles, which John answered the best he could. His Spanish language skills quickly returned.

He then enquired about the situation with the Waps invasion in the continent of Sevilla. He received a litany of terrible stories. While the military situation had stabilized, they were now ensconced in a ring around the city of Sevilla. It was a constant and desperate battle. There were frequent incursions, especially from tunnels underground. The Erch would tunnel in and break out in strength, and there would be a desperate battle to regain lost ground. It was becoming clear that the Erch were doing this more to get food than to gain ground, as they dragged back any human and Erch bodies they got hold of. The troops were getting disheartened. Most of the civilians had been evacuated. But the military were desperately hanging on, because they knew that if the continent of Sevilla was captured, the Erch would turn their attention to the other continents of Arieta. Arieta would be lost.

Finally there were speeches. John was praised fulsomely for being the one most responsible for saving Arieta, by bringing Waps to their aid, and also stimulating help from the Earth government. John felt very embarrassed to there all this. Then John was asked to speak, as "The person who told the fleet, "All humanity expects you to do your duty". The man who has done his duty for Arieta – José Fernadez!" There were loud cheers.

John noticed all the TV cameras tuning in on him. He stood up. "My friends, Citizens of Arieta. Thank you for your too kind words. I have only done what I have done to do what I can to help the Waps and to help save the human race! But we are in a desperate situation. Things are very bad. We must not let the Erch take over this fair planet. They will kill, eat, yes eat, your families as well as you!" There was silence.

John continued. "I know what many of you are thinking. If things get bad, I will get my family on a ship! Well, I have bad news for you. That is not possible. How many millions are there on Arieta? There are not enough ships in the galaxy to carry you away." There was stunned silence. John raised his voice and pitch, hammering the table. "You must stand and fight, every one of you, every man and woman, or watch you families, your loved ones, go down the maws of the Erch." The entire audience stood and screamed, "Kill the Erch. Kill the Erch."

John continued. He was really enjoying this. "I have been told that things are getting desperate in Sevilla. There is no reason to be disconsolate." He waited. "As many of you know I have here on Arieta in a bank vault a ton of gold." He paused. "I offer a kilo of gold for every fresh head of an Erch! One kilo!" He hammered the table and waved his arms, shouting. "I will go to the city of Sevilla myself and make this offer, and set up a mechanism for its instant delivery. Every soldier, civilian, or whoever, who brings me a head of an Erch," and John hammered on the table, "gets from me or my agent a kilo of gold!"

"This war will turn. The Erch will become the hunted. They will be chased from one end of Arieta to another! No Erch will be left on this fair planet, within, within, five years. I promise you!"

There was another screaming standing ovation. "And if you think a tonne of gold is not enough, the Waps owe me a lot more. And maybe I can get an undertaking from them to help pay this bounty. We, all the people of Arieta, will succeed!"

"A kilo of gold for every Erch!"

There was tumult. Women and men were crying. The entire room was screaming and yelling. The bedlam seemed to go on and on.

John sat down, and began thinking, “Do I get any dessert after all this?”

A couple of days later, John together with the President, who did not want to be outdone, landed in Sevilla. John had asked if his old compradore Alfredo Aguirrez could be found, and John was promised that he would meet him on landing at Sevilla. The compradore and his family had survived.

It was a much changed place, though the first thing he found were several piles of Erch heads. John immediately asked for paper, and announced “Please can the owners of these heads put them into separate piles.” After much scurrying and this was done.

John went to the first pile and announced “I have not got the gold with me.” He saw faces fall. “But my paper is as good as gold. Gold will be transported here to exchange for this paper, or you can go to the bank in Merida to exchange it for gold.” There was a lot more interest in the eyes of those in front of him.

He asked, “How many heads in this pile?”

“Ten, senor.”

He wrote, “Please pay the bearer of this note ten kilos of gold.” and he signed the note, José Fernandez, and handed it to the man.

He went down all the piles of heads, handing out similar notes. He then ordered, "Place all these heads in a single pile and burn them. I don't want to buy them again."

John was then quickly escorted round. It was obvious that the defenders were in a desperate state, though the Marine's esprit de corps had kept them from cracking.

He gave the Marines a little speech. "Fellers. You are going to be rich. My offer of a kilo of gold for every Erch head extends to you also. I don't mind how you distribute the loot. But my only proviso is that it is distributed equally, between officers and men. All ranks in Sevilla get the same. Whether individual fighting units get more, and admin troops get less, it is up to you decide. But I want a distribution which the men on the ground consider fair. You understand? Otherwise I shall, I will, start kicking senior heads. I mean that."

The little homily was greeted with smiles.

Finally he met up with Alfredo Aguirrez. He looked much thinner, and his cheek had caved in. His eyes looked hunted. "How is your family, ... ?"

"We have survived," he replied. "I was in prison when the Erch landed. At first they would not let us out. Then the guards fled. We got out. Fortunately my family was two day's walk away, away from the Erch. I managed to reach them in time. As you recommended we had an air car hidden, with a lot of fuel. And a lot of cash. We escaped to Sevilla. But the authorities wanted all the aircars. That night we fled, as the Erch were landing. We took the route you took, to the mountains, where we hid. But the Erch came. We managed to find a fuel station in the extreme north. The fool was willing to take our money. We fled over the sea, island hopping and buying fuel where we could until we reached the main continent. Living there has been difficult. But we survived."

"Well, Alfredo, I am re-hiring you. In fact, you have always been hired. You will get your back pay soon. But this is what I want you to do. I want you to be the man who counts the heads and pays the gold. We will set up a system to help you. But you will write a note that can be exchanged for gold, and sign for it. One kilo of gold for each head. Do you understand?"

Alfredo licked his lips. "Si Senor."

"We will get people to help you. The heads must be destroyed so that you don't pay for them twice. But only you can sign for the gold."

"We will make a banker of you yet," continued John, clapping Alfredo on the shoulders.

John obtained the services of the ex-manager of his bank in Sevilla, and asked him to hire staff for the "Gold Payment Office." The bank's branch in Sevilla was closed, but John sold one ten kilo bar for a pile of currency for salaries and expenses, transferring the rest of the gold bars to Sevilla. There was publicity when the gold bars arrived, and there was a rush to cash the notes. But pretty soon he noticed that people were not cashing the notes, preferring to hold onto them. John had an idea and asked the bank manager to set up a gold account facility, and soon there was a steady trickle of people setting up accounts. John found that after a while people were only cashing a fraction of the notes, and even re-depositing the gold. "I will be a banker yet," thought John.

John had discussed the gold situation with Fred, who had arrived for a visit. John insisted that he did not stay long, as the place was not good for Fred's health. "My guess is that we will need ten thousand kilos of gold," he said.

"There are a lot more Erch out there than that," said Fred.

"Undoubtedly, but this is another lesson for you like double entry accounting. I don't think the Waps have banks. Well in the human sphere, I can issue notes to many times the amount of gold I have, as long as there is confidence that if any individual demands their gold, they would get it. In the normal course of behavior, most people will prefer to hold the notes or keep their accounts and not ask for the gold."

"What happens if they all demand their gold at one time?" asked Fred. "This system is very illogical."

"That happens from time to time. That is called a crisis of confidence or a financial crisis. But the benefits of this system exceed the risks, so humans prefer to continue this system."

Fred hummed a bit. "I cannot understand the logic, but if you say the system is beneficial, there could be benefits to it."

"Now the people who do this are called bankers. They can do this because these people are reputed to be very rich and people have confidence in their financial strength. I am one of these to these people. If I announce I have ten thousand kilos of gold that I will put towards this process, and it is seen to be delivered, they will have even more confidence in me. Indeed fewer people will cash their notes. Now Fred, how much gold do I have do my credit?"

"John, your credit with us is unlimited. We will happily supply you with ten thousand kilos of gold for this purpose, which is for killing Erch."

"I am very glad to hear that. Please could you supply it as soon as possible. You can have the gold back at any time if you want it."

"It is yours. We are very grateful to you," replied Fred.

"One last thing. Can I also put on these notes "Payment in gold guaranteed by the Waps Government" ?"

"Why?"

"It will improve the credit of these notes even more. Essentially all you are saying is that you will pay a kilo of gold for every Erch head, without needing to pay it immediately. I will pay the first ten thousand kilos."

"I think I understand. I agree. Your contributions on the working of human society is very valuable indeed. I will pass this information back. You are accumulating credit faster than the Erch arrive." Fred seemed to laugh.

John smiled wryly.

It was soon found that the Erch head was not enough. The Erch had the habit of dragging their bodies back. John suspected to eat. They also dragged any human bodies back as well. They even tunneled underground to the mass burial sites and stole those bodies. The Erch were obviously short of food, and this more and more colored Erch activities.

The Erch were good tunnellers. They dug tunnels under the defenses, erupted in strength, attacked, and then dragged all the bodies, alive and dead, back into the holes. This had a severe effect on morale, even of the Marines. The arrival of the gold cheered everyone up, and the humans became a lot more aggressive, fighting to kill as many Erch as possible. People were even volunteering to fight in Sevilla. The city began to hold.

Fred was pleased with the palpable change in direction. "We never managed to hold them. If you manage to overcome the Erch, we will be very, very, pleased. Ten thousand kilos of gold will be a small fraction of your credit with us. I will have those gold bars sent to you direct from the Line. But don't get killed. We need you for far more."

"I'll try not to, Fred. But with your permission, I intend to stay here a while longer. They need me. I intend to set up a system which works, where all the Erch are eradicated from the continent of Sevilla."

"You intend to stay that long?"

"No. Only until the tide has clearly been reversed. I am also regaining my strength and health. I am happy here, though it is a war zone. Remember Sevilla is my home. But if you need me, Fred, I shall come."

"I am happy to hear that. You are plainly enjoying yourself. I shall leave you for a while," Fred replied.

They shook hands with every sign of mutual affection.

John proceeded to make sure his bank was working. His credit notes, though signed by Alfredo, had his name and the Waps guarantee on them. They soon began to trade with a premium back at Merida, especially when the ten thousand kilos of gold arrived.

John made sure all the Erch bodies were incinerated in piles near the perimeter of the defenses. This clearly upset the Erch, especially when the black smoke drifted over their side. Human remains were transported back to Merida, for as John said, they only attracted the Erch.

Civilians began arriving to fight the Erch, and claim the gold. As the regular army, both the Marines and the Arietan military did not want much to do with them, John took it on himself to start organizing them into companies. He said, "Go and join an existing company, or if they do not want you, get a dozen of you get together and elect a leader. I will arm and feed you. There is no shortage of Erch." John began recruiting on the other continents, and paying for their transport to Sevilla.

The initial recruits were callow. John provided them with weapons and food, and a brief training. The weapons were plentiful enough. Indeed the Erch weapons, once understood, proved excellent, and became a preferred weapon and something of a status symbol.

The initial casualties were high, but the irregulars soon learned. They found that if they camped near the lines, the Erch would dig under, erupt and massacre them. He got them to camp where there was something solid underneath, such as a concrete car park. He also found that they needed something to rally around in the initial confusion. He started giving each company a flag of their own choice, and trained them to collect around it, firing outwards until help arrived. He devised rules for division of the loot among all participants, encouraged the men to start accounts so that if they were killed their families would get their gold, rather than having the notes stolen from their bodies.

Imperceptibly he began to be regarded as the leader of all the irregulars. "El Caudillo do Sevilla," or just "El Caudillo." He became as powerful a person as the leader of the military, which happened to be a General of the Marines. But John did not put on airs, and tried to be as cordial and cooperative with the military as possible.

The tide began to turn. The attacks under the perimeter became less frequent. Then John noticed that the Erch began to tunnel to the cellars under the buildings in the center of the city, making the city again unsafe. He began installing Erch alarms in all the cellars, with an alarm on the surface nearby. He also began to allocate blocks to different companies, who had the first opportunity to go after those Erch. By now the men needed no urging. There was a get rich quick mentality among every man. Every incursion was met with explosions, shooting, and then silence, as the Erch bodies were dragged out for counting, and their own casualties hauled away.

The companies began to live in the buildings in the city center. John felt they were being a bit too confident, but it was more comfortable than living in the middle of a car park. John continued to live in the main square. He felt safe with solid stone under him.

But one night every cellar of the city filled up. Alarms sounded everywhere. There was confusion in the buildings. Next, the Erch commenced a completely new tactic. They blew away the ceiling, and erupted into the floor above, grabbing the men who fell screaming into their claws. The Erch continued doing this, climbing higher and higher. The more sensible men headed for the roof, out of cowardice or level-headedness. Those on the high buildings survived until morning, crowded together on the roofs. Those men on the collapsed levels had completely disappeared, along with the Erch.

It was a major disaster. The military commander was openly gloating. But it was only temporary. John intensified his recruitment, and rebuilt the strength of the irregulars. This time he had a plan. Every night he camped his men on the roofs of every building, rebuilding those roofs that had collapsed. They were carried up there by aircars. He removed the lower floors so that the Erch could not climb up. He placed alarms near the entrance holes of the Erch. And waited.

During the day the men spread out, moving through the suburbs, searching for Erch. By this time they had pretty effective Erch detectors. At night if any Erch breakout was detected aircars descended on the Erch, and they made sure that the Erch could not drag the Erch bodies away. John felt that this must be having an effect on them.

One night, all the alarms in the center of the city erupted simultaneously. As they had been trained, the men moved to the edge of the roofs and waited. The Erch erupted simultaneously from the buildings and onto the street. The men began firing. The Erch tried to fire back. But the intensity of fire from the humans above mowed them down. Soon the remnants of the Erch were in the sides of the building firing upwards, but with limited effect. Spot fire from above eliminated them. Any attempt by the Erch to drag a body back was prevented.

The firing died down later in the night, leaving a deep pile of Erch bodies up and down all the streets and avenues. Dawn showed a total massacre, and the Erch were soon eliminated from all the cellars. Nearly twenty thousand Erch were killed.

"Good thing I am a bank," thought John. In consultation with the leaders of the companies and the military, the gold was distributed equitably. The Erch bodies burned for days.

After that there were few attacks. John thought, "As soon as the men start getting bored and stroppy, I will ask for an extension of the perimeter."

And sure enough, he soon received a delegation from the companies.

As he said to the General, "I think the last defeat has vastly reduced the Erch numbers and resources. I am willing to pay for a new perimeter five hundred meters further out."

"And retain the old perimeter?" the General asked.

"Yes. I think it is best to retain two perimeters, and leapfrog out. We will widen the perimeters one at a time until we cover all the continent."

"That will take a long time."

"I don't think so. We can speed the process up later by widening the distance between the perimeters. But I feel it is necessary to make sure that no Erch are left behind the lines."

The widening of the perimeter proceeded gradually. Initially there was resistance, and the military forces got good rewards in gold. But the resistance began to die out. From time to time they came across a nest. John announced that young Erch had the same price, but the military soon learned not to go down into them. The Waps announced that they had a suitable gas, and conducted the gassing of these nests with a great deal of apparent pleasure. As Fred said, "I don't know what your reservations are. These are Erch."

"Our feelings are there are young down there," replied John.

"But they grow into adult Erch. From your point of you there can be no redemption for them," replied Fred.

CHAPTER EIGHTEEN

Long before the perimeter reached the ocean to the north, John was called back to the ship. By this time he had achieved a swaggering persona, with a beard, an open shirt, a red bandana on his head, and leather boots. He was always followed around by the media and a small crowd, who listened to every word.

He announced, "I have to return to the ship now. I am leaving you in good hands. Alfredo Aguirrez is in charge of the Gold Payment Office, and I know he will do a good job. The Waps promise an unlimited supply of gold in order to eliminate the Erch." Load cheers. "I leave the irregular companies in charge of Raymondo Bartelo, an experienced fighter. He will be your new Caudillo." Groans. "But I shall return! The continent of Sevilla will be a safe place. I, my wife and children will return to Sevilla to live!" Cheers. "A reconstructed and rebuilt city and continent of Sevilla!" Load cheers.

He returned to Merida to have a very cordial farewell with the President and his Cabinet. "The tide is turned. The Erch will certainly be wiped from Sevilla and Arieta. They will be destroyed. Every one of them. And thanks to the Waps, Arieta will be enriched in the process. More than enough to rebuild."

"And thanks to you!" exclaimed the President. "We do not know how to thank you. As a small token, we bestow on you our highest honor, the medal and sash of Saint Simion." And in front of a small crowd of officials, he bestowed a large crimson sash with gold borders on John, with a large spiky medal attached. The assembled group broke into applause.

"My gratitude to all of you. I take this medal on behalf of the citizens of Arieta who fought bravely by my side, many dying. If it was not for them, I would not have achieved the success I did," replied John truthfully.

John was persuaded to take a farewell public dinner, which he accepted gratefully, and attended wearing the sash and medal over his formal clothes. The speech that night went as follows. "Friends, people of Arieta, I bring you good news. The Erch are being thrown back and destroyed. Soon the perimeter fence will reach the sea and will soon be extended over all the continent of Sevilla!" Loud cheers, people jumped out of their chairs, stood on them, threw him flowers, blew him kisses. """I do not claim credit for this." Oh! "Yes it was the brave people of Arieta, as well as the courageous Space Marines, who gave their lives to destroy the Erch!" Cheers. "My friends, many of you will no doubt have the question, whether I shall continue to pay gold for the dead Erch? The answer is, yes I will! I will continue to do this forever. Furthermore these notes are guaranteed by the Waps. They guarantee unlimited gold for the dead Erch, with no time limit!" John thumped the table. "I am sure that many of you used to go hunting. I am sure all the Sevillan creatures in those forests will be dead. But remember, if brave persons go into those woods to hunt Erch, they will get a kilo of gold for each one. More valuable than some meat or a skin!"

John collected his breathe and waited. "I now have to go onto a serious administrative and political issue." He looked around. "When the perimeter was extended it became apparent that all that land inside and outside the perimeter was a wasteland. Lets face it, most of the owners of those farms, those properties, are dead. All their most distant relations are dead. Grass and weeds grow everywhere." The audience looked at each other.

"It is vitally necessary that this farm land, this urban property, must be brought back to productive use as soon as possible. The property must be transferred to new living owners, who will be required to bring the land back to use within a set time. Leave it like it is, and the land will be open to speculation and corruption, and there will be no end of trouble. I suggest that that a body, which I call the "Land Redemption Commission," be set up. I suggest that open and honest rules are set up. Living owners of all Sevillan land must be searched for or advertised for in a set time. If no-one is found, the property must be openly auctioned, with the requirement that if it is farming land it to brought back to production in a certain time, or if urban property, brought back to productive use. If we do not do this, the land will be taken over by the scheming crooks who hang around the edges of all governments. So set up a "Land Redemption Commission" immediately. The consequences if you do not do this, though tempting, will prove extremely painful, if not fatal for many of you. Do not act dishonestly. There is no protection. There is too much at stake, economically and politically."

"That is all I have to say. I wish you all every success. In the words of a historic warrior, I shall return!" Tremendous cheers and clapping. Shouts of Viva! Viva!

After more speeches, and a night's rest at the hotel, he was transported between cheering and enthusiastic crowds to the spaceport. He could hear the words, "Caudillo! Caudillo!"

"I could get used to this," he thought.

He was rapidly transported by shuttle to the ship, where Fred met him. It was a different ship. "We have better accommodation for you," said Fred. And indeed it was. A comfortable suite, with comfortable furniture. A separate bathroom with a human toilet. "And we have a shower for you," said Fred. And indeed they had. John just giggled.

CHAPTER NINETEEN

John had never been in such a tremendous city in his life. He understood why Earth's two biggest combined problems were the generation of excess heat from human activity and the insufficient generation of new oxygen. Even with strict population controls the population kept rising. Outside the high-rise cities every square inch was green, and indeed the oceans were seeded with nutrients so that all the surfaces were green. Nevertheless, even though the population had moved away from the equatorial regions, and way up north and south, it was still warm. Here in Moscow, the Federation capital, the air was muggy and John found it difficult to breathe. He understood why the wealthy carried around inconspicuous tubes transferring oxygen into their nostrils. The better hotels and offices were "oxygen enhanced", as well as air conditioned, which he appreciated.

John was treated as royalty, and located in a luxury hotel suite. His every whim was supplied. Apparently the Waps had been given part of a high-rise building for their Embassy, which they had converted to their own needs. Among other things they found the atmosphere too damp for themselves, and the inside of what had become their Embassy was dry and warm. John was offered accommodation there, but decided it was too much trouble for the Waps to create a separate environment. "They'll go out of their way to build me a shower," he thought. "They seem obsessive about that. It must be my body odor." As it was, he showered twice a day, and felt he needed it.

Negotiations had started. John had expected this and said the Waps, "If you let it, these negotiations will drag on and useful results will be slow to achieve. I suggest that we make a priority of setting up the system of the Joint Committee, and the Arbitration Committee. Then when this has been done, you think up a list of things you want to discuss. We will give these people a list and begin to discuss them one by one. Then when the discussions get bogged down, we refer each item to the Joint Committee. If there is no resolution to the matter within say thirty days, we refer it to the Arbitration Committee. This way, the issues and differences will be clarified on the way down, and the final decision will be made by the Arbitrator."

"Do you think it will work?" asked one of the Waps.

"Yes, if you nail down the agreement that the Arbitrator's decision is final. The senior negotiators will soon learn that you are taking all the decision-making away from them, and won't like it. They will seek to change certain Arbitrator's decisions. Just discuss the matter again to clarify the issues, refer it again to the Joint Committee, which if it obfuscates, will have the matter referred again to the Arbitration Committee. They will soon learn that reversals will be rare, and they will be wasting their time stringing the negotiations out. What is worse they will be losing their power. In a matter of months all negotiations at the highest level will proceed smoothly, and the Joint Committee and the Arbitration Committee will have little to do."

"I see, ingenious as usual," said the Waps.

"The system must include a reason for referring contentious decisions to the Joint Committee. I suggest initially putting a time limit of one week on each issue before referring it to the Joint Committee."

"What about more urgent issues?"

"In those cases, refer them directly to the Joint Committee, or if very urgent to the Arbitrator."

"What if they do not follow the agreed decisions."

"Here is the difficult one. You must impose penalties and indemnities at a rising level of severity. Ranging from embarrassing to downright painful. Somewhere in between the humans will come to their senses. Remember, in every case of non-compliance, it is usually a single individual who is recalcitrant. No person has total power. Long before you raise the penalty to a very painful level, the collective influence of the others, especially those who are losing, will prevail. I will advise you on this, and make sure you don't step into areas that will induce total resistance. These are called 'motherhood' issues, which are rare. But you are strongly advised that when I say don't, you stop immediately, and find another way."

"Can you give an example of such an issue?"

"Hmmmm……The Waps announce that they want a change of diet and want a supply of human babies," John said. The Waps began to hum discordantly. "Look I was only joking. There are core issues the humans will not cede. Territory is one of them. Don't ever demand a human world, regardless of how much milk you need."

"I understand. However that joke was upsetting to us," the Waps said.

"I understand. It was because I did not understand you well enough."

"We are very similar in many respects, despite being physically different," observed Fred.

"I am glad to hear that. I am sure we will get on well," John replied.

And they did. The humans and the Waps began to get on famously. As soon as the humans grew to respect the Waps, and learned that they could not "negotiate" advantages, their relationship developed into mutual trust. Commercial relationships developed. Based on "The Line" protocols – ie all disputes were referred to the peculiar arbitration system. The legal profession and the judges hated it, and waxed long and hard about the injustice of it all, but the rule was "If you want to deal with the Waps, ALL disputes go to arbitration." Pretty soon, it was amazing how many commercial deals managed to include at least one Waps. The courts were being by-passed and short circuited. Soon additional Waps-Human Arbitration Courts were being set up on every planet.

One night, after returning from a pretty knotty and convoluted discussion, John was in his hotel room, preparing for his regular shower. He heard a soft tap on the door. "I'm sure I have heard that tap before he thought," as he strode to the door and opened it.

"Gwen! And the kids! And a baby! What the….! Come in!"

He grabbed Gwen, and kissed her over the smelly little bundle that was staring up at him. The kids yelled and started pulling at him.

Gwen immediately said. "Did you get my letters?"

"No, darling, no!" John replied.

"Well," she said, looking a bit guilty, "you know I was pregnant just before you left. I got very worried about you. Hearing about all those battles."

"But you received my letters. I was perfectly safe!" replied John not quite truthfully. "And I told you to stay at The Line. You and the kids were safe there. The Waps were looking after you."

"I know. But I didn't want to have the baby on my own," Gwen replied.

"I understand darling. But you could have had the baby at a hospital on the human side of the line. No-one would have dared touch you."

"Well, anyway," Gwen continued defiantly, "I had begun again to write to my parents. Remember you had forbade that when we were on Arieta. Now everyone knew where we were it did not matter. So I wrote to them. And they wrote back."

She took a breath and looked down guiltily.

"I thought I would like to have the baby at home, at Cymru, my home planet, with my parents, instead of that alien place." She rushed on. "They loved to have me, and they loved to see the children. We had a lovely time. And the birth was no problem."

"You went to Cymru? How?"

Well.... The kind Mr Johannes Albrecht put his private space ship at my disposal. It was very kind of him. And the trip did not take long."

"Oh..." replied John.

"And I greatly enjoyed my stay at Cymru. Seeing my old friends, and home again," Gwen rushed on. "My parents just loved to see me again. And the children. I was waited on hand and foot. And the birth went very well. The baby is normal and very healthy. Mum and dad were so pleased."

"Then we heard you were on Earth. I remembered that I missed you terribly! So I decided to take a ship straight here! First class! Luxury! Everybody bowed and scraped when they learned who I was!"

"Well, no harm done. I love to see you again. I have been missing you like crazy. And what is this little one's name?"

"She is called Elwyn, is that all right with you? She is three months old and a perfect darling."

The baby sniffled a bit.

Then there was another knock on the door. "Damn," said John. "I wish the staff would leave me alone."

He opened the door.

A man stood there holding a gun. Two men stood behind him also holding guns.

"Rick!" squeaked Gwen.

"Yes, its me. How are you, darling?" he asked sarcastically, pushing in to the room. The other two men followed.

"What are you doing here? I thought you were in prison!" Gwen squeaked.

"They let me out. So I came after you," Rick answered.

"Why?" Gwen asked.

"Because I want you. I love you. And I am going to have you!"

"But I don't love you," Gwen answered.

"You will learn to love me."

"No I won't. You were horrid to me. You hurt me," Gwen said.

"I am sorry about that. I thought you were chasing after other men," Rick replied.

"But you didn't own me," said Gwen.

"But I do now," Rick said, smiling grimly and raising his gun.

"No, you don't!" shouted Gwen.

"After I have dealt with this bastard, I will take you away and teach you to love me," shouted Rick. He turned his gun on John.

Gwen screamed, "No you don't." She jumped in front of John. She yelled, "If you hurt John and the children I will kill myself!"

John intervened, and said, "You guys," talking to the two other men, "I am a Waps diplomat. If you kill me you will be tracked down, taken to The Line, put in a glass case, and shot!" Their guns wavered and eyes rolled.

Rick's face grimaced. He paused and said, "I have a better idea. You are coming with me. With the others. Move it." And he pointed to a lift that had a direct connection to the aircar landing pad on the roof. He waved his gun again.

The other men moved forward and began prodding and shoving John and Gwen. John gathered the children and they moved slowly to the door of the lift. They entered and Rick pressed the button for the roof.

He said "Convenient, hey? We have a car waiting on the roof."

The door slid open on the roof. It was dark and windy. The warm and muggy air gusted around them. The car waited there in the dark. "Forward," said Rick.

They took about five steps forward. Then three red beams shot out, felling the three men. Out of the gloom stepped a number of Waps. One of them was Fred.

"We have studied human physiology, and none on them could contract their finger when we shot them," Fred said.

"Oh, Fred!" cried Gwen.

"Am I glad to see you," said John.

"We knew something was wrong when the human guards on your level was shot. We had a monitor on them at all times. Then we viewed the monitors on your floor and in your suite. We saw what was happening. By that time our aircar had left the embassy, and was landing on the roof. We had made preparations for this eventuality. We killed the driver of their car, and hid in the dark. We know that humans cannot see well in the dark, and we destroyed the lights. When you left the lifts, it was just a matter of shooting simultaneously when the assailants were at an optimal location."

"Well, you are obviously dead shots," replied John.

"We have extremely accurate fine motor skills," replied Fred, sounding proud. "Now let us return to your suite and discuss the arrival of Gwen and the children."

"What about these…?" asked John, pointing at the bodies.

"We shall draw the human authorities attention to them, and demand a clear explanation for their presence."

"I bet you will. Rick could not wander around without connivance at a high level."

Inside the suite Fred said, "I am happy to see you again, Gwen, and your children. I see that you have another one. I assume that it is John's child also."

Gwen colored a bit. "Yes it is. Across the Line it was not possible for another man to inseminate me." She was used to Fred's strange questions.

John smiled broadly. Gwen looked him hard in the eye.

"Well, said Fred, addressing Gwen, "the question is now what to do with you. As you can see, despite our best efforts, security is not very good here. We had learned of Rick's release from prison, and when you travelled to Cymru, we asked Johannes Albrecht to keep you safe. Rick was apprehended on Cymru and made to leave the planet. Unfortunately your sudden decision to leave Cymru for Earth was not communicated to us in time, and our assumption that your security arrangements would follow you to Earth proved false. Our knowledge of your arrival at this hotel occurred at the same time that we were appraised that Rick had killed a guard. This is most unfortunate. Our security arrangements, we see know, concentrated on the safety of John. You are we could call our Achilles heel."

"What do you suggest now?" asked John.

"I suggest that all of you move straight away to the embassy. We have prepared a human suite for this eventuality. But it is small for a large human family. I have already communicated with the Waps High Command. I would like to transport Gwen and the children back to the Line. They will be safe there."

"What? I have only just arrived. I will have no time with John," Gwen complained.

"It is entirely up to you. But we can allow one night together. At the Embassy. This whole hotel area will soon, as you say, be crawling with police."

Gwen looked devastated, and John hugged her. "Come on, it is all for the best."

They went back up to the roof, entered an aircar, and were rapidly carried to the Embassy.

"Here is the human suite. You should find it quite comfortable. As you see we even have a shower," Fred said.

John stamped his foot. Gwen smiled at John, and toted Elwyn into the room.

The triumphal procession in Sevilla about four years later was overwhelming. It was led by military bands, a corps of Marines and units of the Arietan army. Then irregulars, assorted politicians in their open cars, including the Governor of Sevilla and the President of Arieta. The crowd screamed and cheered, and tossed flowers at all those in the parade.

Then John appeared, together with his wife. The crowd went ecstatic. The police could hardly control them. They screamed and shouted, and his car was covered in a rain of flowers.

"José, José, José Fernadez" they yelled, and threatened to engulf his car.

As the flowers kept falling in the car, John turned to Gwen and said "Whisper in my ear the words "Hominem te momento". Keep whispering it."

Gwen smiled, leant forward and whispered "Hominem te momento. And I love you darling."

www.ingramcontent.com/pod-product-compliance
Lightning Source LLC
Chambersburg PA
CBHW060104260626
47160CB00005B/1800

* 9 7 8 0 9 8 7 4 9 4 6 2 7 *